Nordic Terrors

ANTHEM STUDIES IN GOTHIC LITERATURE

Anthem Studies in Gothic Literature incorporates a broad range of titles that undertake rigorous, multidisciplinary and original scholarship in the domain of Gothic Studies and respond, where possible, to existing classroom/module needs. The series aims to foster innovative international scholarship that interrogates established ideas in this rapidly growing field, to broaden critical and theoretical discussion among scholars and students, and to enhance the nature and availability of existing scholarly resources.

Series Editor
Carol Margaret Davison – University of Windsor, Canada

Nordic Terrors

Scandinavian Superstition in British Gothic Literature

Robert W. Rix

ANTHEM PRESS

Anthem Press
An imprint of Wimbledon Publishing Company
www.anthempress.com

This edition first published in UK and USA 2025
by ANTHEM PRESS
75–76 Blackfriars Road, London SE1 8HA, UK
or PO Box 9779, London SW19 7ZG, UK
and
244 Madison Ave #116, New York, NY 10016, USA

British Library Cataloguing-in-Publication Data
A catalogue record for this book is available from the British Library.

Library of Congress Cataloging-in-Publication Data
A catalog record for this book has been requested.
2024937591

ISBN-13: 978-1-83999-045-8 (Pbk)
ISBN-10: 1-83999-045-7 (Pbk)

Cover Credit: Caspar David Friedrich - Winterlandschaft mit Kirche/
wikimedia commons

This title is also available as an e-book.

CONTENTS

INTRODUCTION

Geographic location is a vital component in British Gothic literature, and the location of Gothic fiction has been of perennial interest among critics.[1] If one looks at the Gothic locations chosen by British writers, including Horace Walpole, Ann Radcliffe, Matthew Lewis and a host of imitative Minerva Press novelists, Southern Europe was a popular setting. From a British Protestant perspective, the perception of Catholicism was adversarial, shaped by the cultural, religious, and political climate of the eighteenth and nineteenth centuries. Cannon Schmitt has coined the term 'alien nation' to describe Gothic texts that establish a location culturally opposite to the writer's position, helping to conceptualise a sense of national identity.[2] Further afield in fictional space, William Beckford's Islamic Arabo-Persian setting in *Vathek* (1786) capitalises on the British fascination with Oriental settings. We may observe how the legends and mythology associated with these places are made vehicles of terror and the supernatural. However, it would be a critical cliché to confine the genre to just fantasised regions abroad; English and Scottish locations are also found in the early Gothic novels of Clara Reeve and James Hogg. Within these locales, one can observe that Gothic narratives are often intertwined with local legends and tales related to the setting. To borrow a formulation from Catherine Spooner and Emma McEvoy about Gothic texts, it is a discernible tendency that 'space characteristically becomes historicised and history becomes spatialised'.[3]

The focus of this book is on Nordic culture and its association with Anglophone Gothic texts. A key argument I will present is that the familiar concept of

---

1 *Gothic Topographies: Language, Nation-Building and 'Race'*, ed. Paivi Mehtonen and Matti Savolainen (Farnham: Ashgate, 2016) is a wide-ranging collection on this subject.

2 Cannon Schmitt, *Alien Nation: Nineteenth-Century Gothic Fictions and English Nationality* (Philadelphia, PA: University of Pennsylvania Press, 1997).

3 Catherine Spooner and Emma McEvoy, 'Gothic Locations', in *The Routledge Companion to Gothic*, ed. Catherine Spooner and Emma McEvoy (repr. London: Routledge, 2009), 51–53 (52).

the Gothic 'Other' becomes difficult to uphold in relation to Nordic terror. This is because writers saw the Nordic tradition as a part of their own cultural and ethnic history. Nordic pagan religion and folklore were seen not only to preserve cultural elements of a broader Germanic ethnic heritage but also to represent a direct lineage to the British past, as Scandinavians were known to have settled in Britain. I propose that British writers tackled the depiction of Nordic terrors as an element in a complex discussion about their historical heritage and the part it played in shaping the contemporary nation. However, the strong connection to British history does not necessarily make the utilisation of Nordic tradition more reliable than the depictions of Catholic or Oriental beliefs. The general trend when Nordic tradition is Gothicised is that it becomes reconstructed in highly selective, exaggerated and hyperbolic versions. This is a process not dissimilar to Edward Said's well-known concept of 'Orientalism'.

This book argues that Nordic terror became a recognisable marker in literary texts in ways not dissimilar to the term 'German'. So-called 'German' stories encompassed both literary output translated from German and English works that used German settings, such as Eliza Parsons' *The Castle of Wolfenbach* (1793), which was subtitled 'A German Story'. Thus, 'German' became a national denominator that functioned as a market ploy for advertising stories that relied on terror.[4] While 'German' was a loose sub-genre term for Gothic writing, Nordic Gothic often directly references mythology or legendary history. *Nordic Terrors: Scandinavian Superstition in British Gothic Literature* provides an in-depth analysis of the influence of Nordic supernaturalism on British literature. I aim to highlight the significance of Nordic themes and motifs in shaping what became an alternative mode of Gothic and survey its evolution in poetry and novels from the late eighteenth to the early nineteenth centuries. This analysis will demonstrate how Nordic mythology and folklore, sometimes argued to be imported to Britain with the incursions of Scandinavians who became settlers, played a significant role in the ongoing negotiation of British history and national identity.

In recent years, there has been an increasing interest in how Nordic superstition is worked into texts written in the Scandinavian languages. Yvonne Leffler's book *Swedish Gothic: Landscapes of Untamed Nature* (2022) demonstrates that modern Gothic literature in Swedish incorporates the local folklore of trolls, *tomtes* or *vittras*.[5] The collected volume *Nordic Gothic* (2020) has a broader remit, exploring how figures from Nordic folklore become

---

4 See Patrick Bridgewater, *The German Gothic Novel in Anglo-German Perspective* (Amsterdam: Rodopi, 2013), esp. 451–54.
5 Yvonne Leffler, *Swedish Gothic: Landscapes of Untamed Nature* (London: Anthem Press, 2022).

metaphorical representations in Scandinavian texts and other media from the 1990s onwards.[6] In contrast to these works, the present book examines late eighteenth- and early nineteenth-century texts in English. Several studies detail the reception of Norse tradition in British literature, dating back to F. E. Farley's *Scandinavian Influences in the English Romantic Movement* (1903). More recently, Margaret Clunies Ross' *The Norse Muse in Britain 1750–1820* (1998), Andrew Wawn's *The Vikings and the Victorians: Inventing the Old North in Nineteenth-Century Britain* (2000), Heather O'Donoghue's *English Poetry and Old Norse Myth: A History* (2014) and *Studies in the Transmission and Reception of Old Norse Literature: The Hyperborean Muse in European Culture* (2016), edited by Judy Quinn and Maria Adele Cipolla, have extended the critical appraisal.[7] These excellent studies provide valuable analyses of the highways and byways of the reception. However, no studies have exclusively focused on Nordic terrors were activated for Gothic reading.[8] The critical vacuum motivates the present book.

An important consideration when analysing the literary and cultural discourses surrounding Nordic tradition in the eighteenth and nineteenth centuries is the use of terminology. Specifically, in the context of Nordic Gothic, the term 'Gothic' can be seen to connect the definition of an ethnocultural heritage to what is currently acknowledged as a label for a genre of literature that deals with themes of fear and terror. It is pertinent to unfold this connection here in the introduction. It was commonly claimed that all Germanic nations originated in Scandinavia. This was not least owing to the sixth-century Gothic-Roman historian Jordanes, who had established what became a well-known legend of ancient Scandinavia (*Scandza*) as a *vagina gentium* (womb of nations), from which Europe was populated through migration.[9] The English statesman and essayist Sir William Temple explained in *Introduction to the History of England*

6 *Nordic Gothic*, ed. Maria Holmgren Troy et al. (Manchester: Manchester University Press, 2020).

7 F. E. Farley, *Scandinavian Influences in the English Romantic Movement* (Boston, MA: Ginn & Co., 1903); Margaret Clunies Ross, The Norse Muse in Britain: 1750–1820 (Parnaso: Trieste, 1998), Andrew Wawn, *The Vikings and the Victorians: Inventing the Old North in Nineteenth-Century Britain* (Cambridge: D. S. Brewer, 2000); Heather O'Donoghue, *English Poetry and Old Norse Myth: A History* (Oxford: Oxford University Press, 2014); *Studies in the Transmission and Reception of Old Norse Literature: The Hyperborean Muse in European Culture*, eds. Judy Quinn and Maria Adele Cipolla (Brepols: Turnhout, 2016).

8 A shorter attempt at defining this mode of writing is my 'Gothic Gothicism: Norse Terror in the Late Eighteenth to Early Nineteenth Centuries'. *Gothic Studies* 13, no. 1 (2011): 1–20.

9 For an analysis of how Jordanes was used in England, see Colin Kidd, *British Identities before Nationalism: Ethnicity and Nationhood in the Atlantic World, 1600–1800* (Cambridge: Cambridge University Press, 1999), esp. 216–23.

(1695) that the Anglo-Saxons were 'one branch of those Gothic Nations [...] swarming from the Northern Hive'.[10] *Gothic* had multiple meanings, but one crucial sense was Germanic/Teutonic. However, a specific connection between Scandinavians and Goths was claimed in Britain. In his classical study, Samuel Kliger points out that the translation commissioned by King Alfred of Bede's *Ecclesiastical History of the English People* erroneously rendered the Latin name for the Jutes, one of the invading Germanic tribes in the fifth century, as Goths.[11] Thus, it was suggested that settlers from what is believed to be Danish Jutland were a contingent of Goths.

When it comes to written evidence of the Gothic religion and manners, Icelandic texts were considered the best extant examples. When the scholar Thomas Percy published *Five Pieces of Runic Poetry Translated from the Islandic Language* (1763), he emphasised that Iceland was converted to Christianity much later (only around 1000 CE) than England. For that reason, Icelandic texts preserved their 'original manners and customs longer than any other of the Gothic tribes', and this was long enough to commit their supernatural beliefs to writing.[12] Percy is keen to point out how Icelandic was closely related to Old English and how beliefs, manners and customs expressed in Icelandic texts were shared across 'northern nations', including the pre-Christian Anglo-Saxons.[13] Therefore, when the antiquarian John Brand refers to the belief in witches as 'Gothic or Scandinavian Superstition' in his seminal *Observations on Popular Antiquities* (1777), it is just one example of how these two terms were often used interchangeably to describe what was seen as a single, identifiable culture.[14]

For the literary historian Thomas Warton the notion that Gothic superstition could be found in Britain's ancestral history influenced literary development. In the first volume of *The History of English Poetry* (1774), he argues that Scandinavian Skalds came to Britain with the invasions from the continent in the fifth century and brought their various beliefs with them. As a result, their poetic effusions ensured that 'the old Gothic and Scandinavian superstitions are to this day retained in the English language',

---

10 William Temple, *An Introduction to the History of England* (London: R. & R. Simpson, 1695), 44.

11 Samuel Kliger, *The Goths in England: A Study in Seventeenth and Eighteenth Century Thought* (Cambridge, MA.: Harvard University Press, 1952), 14–15.

12 *Five Pieces of Runic Poetry Translated from the Islandic Language*, ed. and trans. Thomas Percy (London: R. Dodsley, 1763), [ii].

13 Ibid.

14 John Brand and Henry Bourne, *Observations on Popular Antiquities* (London: J. Johnson, 1777), 324.

for example, the concept of the ghostly spirit Mara, 'from whence our Night-mare is derived'.[15] Warton refers to the ethnic category 'Scandinavian Goths', who made 'descents on Britain', and he generally sees texts containing information about Norse mythology as a rich archive of wider ethno-Gothic beliefs.[16]

As a term for a new mode of terror literature, 'Gothic' is used by Horace Walpole for the first time as a label for a mode of literary writing in the second edition of *The Castle of Otranto* (1766). In the preface, he praises Shakespeare as the model he copies for his novel, and the storyline riffs on *Hamlet* insofar as a ghost haunts the castle. Walpole emulated Shakespeare in his creative efforts because the playwright had become established as an English genius who incorporated elements of superstitious folklore into his plays. In doing so, he aspired to craft an original form of novel that would honour the native literary traditions. As Richard Hurd, the vocal eighteenth-century defender of the fantastical in literature, pointed out, Shakespeare adopted 'the *Gothic* system of prodigy and enchantment', and his *Macbeth* contains 'the *Danish* or *Northern*, intermixed with the *Greek* and *Roman* enchantments' commingled with 'our own country superstitions'.[17] Walpole chose to set his 'Gothic' scene in the southern climes of Italy, but he would have been well aware of the term's reference to ancient Northern beliefs, as this had been preserved in Scandinavian mythology. In a letter dated August 1760, Walpole describes Strawberry Hill as a place where he was 'always impatient to be back with my own Woden and Thor, my own Gothic Lares'.[18]

The purpose of the present study is to show that the interest in Nordic traditions permeated a part of the literary Gothic and came to define the very essence of its stylisation and themes. I shall refer to this as Nordic 'terrors'. This is with full awareness that modern critical literature often distinguishes between 'terror' and 'horror', taking a cue from Ann Radcliffe's essay 'On the Supernatural in Poetry', written in 1802 but published posthumously

---

15 Thomas Warton, 'On the Origin of Romantic Fiction in Europe', in *The History of English Poetry, from the Close of the Eleventh to the Commencement of the Eighteenth Century*, vol. 1 (London: J. Dodsley et al., 1774), [xxxix].

16 Ibid., 128.

17 Richard Hurd, *Moral and Political Dialogues; with Letters on Chivalry and Romance*, 5th ed., vol. 3 (London: T. Cadell, 1776), 254, 256. See further, Steven Craig, 'Shakespeare among the Goths', in *Gothic Shakespeares*, ed. John Drakakis and Dale Townshend (Abingdon: Routledge, 2008), 42–59.

18 Cited in Martin Arnold, 'On the Origins of the Gothic Novel: From Old Norse to Otranto', in *Bram Stoker and the Gothic: Formations to Transformations*, ed. Catherine Wynne (Houndsmills: Palgrave, 2016), 14–29 (25).

in 1826. However, supernatural ballad material, which will be discussed below, was most regularly labelled as 'terror', as we see it in Walter Scott's collection *An Apology for Tales of Terror* (1799) and the commercial publication *Tales of Terror* (1801). Both these collections of ballad imitations include pieces connected with Scandinavia. Another point about terminology concerns the terms 'Nordic' and 'Scandinavia'. Today, Scandinavia is usually used narrowly in reference to Denmark, Norway and Sweden, while 'Nordic' refers to the wider area of the North, including the nations of Denmark, Finland, Iceland, Norway and Sweden (as well as the autonomous territories of the Faroe Islands, Greenland and the region of Åland). During the period discussed in this book, 'Scandinavian' was the common term for the whole Nordic cultural area. In fact, 'Nordic' is not recorded in English until 1824.[19] Thus, what we today more accurately would call 'Nordic' would, at the time, be designated as 'Scandinavian'. The main title of this book, 'Nordic Terrors', conveys a modern research agenda, while the subtitle reflects that 'Scandinavian superstition' is the historical theme it explores. However, to avoid any confusion in the main text, I will use the term 'Scandinavian' as an adjective throughout to indicate the historical topic under discussion. However, I give preference to the term 'Norse' (which was in use at the time) in discussions of texts that specifically refer to the medieval mythology contained in the two Eddas, as this most accurately describes this particular tradition.

Having presented the overarching scope of the book, I will now give a short outline of the individual chapters. Chapter 1 explores the cultural reception, reinterpretation and significance of Norse poetry in Britain. I argue that the Norse tradition occupied a somewhat privileged position in the transnational framework of Gothic literature. The chapter examines how interest in Norse poetry was driven by a desire to define cultural lineage and explore an Anglo-Saxon vernacular past, particularly in competition with the popular Ossian poetry. I examine the cultural significance of the terrifying elements of the Icelandic texts and how they were read as proof of the ethnic ancestors' unique bravery in confronting ghosts and the realm of death.

Chapter 2 analyses the translation and adaptation of Danish ballads, discussing their role in creating a literary image of Denmark as a place of terror. Previous studies have largely overlooked this trend in Gothic writing. The primary focus is on Matthew Lewis' collection *Tales of Wonder* (1801),

---

19 *Oxford English Dictionary*, s.v. 'Nordic, adj., sense 1.b', July 2023. https://doi. org/10.1093/OED/6731208065.

in which Danish ballads are translated. I uncover the cultural dynamics behind the transformation of the ballads into Gothic narratives and examine the contradictory and ambiguous presentation of the ballads, ranging from antiquarian approaches to satirical imitations.

Chapter 3 examines the transformations of J. W. Goethe's 'Erlkönig', a ballad inspired by Danish folklore, into various English translations. The second part of the chapter focuses on Matthew Lewis' drama *One O'Clock! Or, The Knight and the Wood Dæmon* (1811), which features a female version of the malignant Scandinavian spirit Goethe had invoked. This shows how Danish superstition also worked transmedially. My argument is that Lewis, in this play for the popular stage, uses Danish folklore as a symbol of the past preventing modernity.

Chapter 4 explores literary works that draw upon Scandinavian superstitions as they had been practised in Britain. If the defeat of superstition in the name of modernity can also be found in poems and novels by Ann Radcliffe and Walter Scott, there is here also a historical recognition that the unruly beliefs formed part of the rich tapestry stitched throughout Britain's history. The past Scandinavian settlers may also have imparted upon the national psyche certain defining attributes – like the spirit of freedom and resilience – still considered cultural ideals. The chapter critically examines the impact of Scandinavian settlers in Britain and how their legacy was remembered and renegotiated in the creation of national identity.

Taken together, the chapters explore how Scandinavian terrors came to occupy a unique position within British Gothic literature. The book demonstrates how the antiquarian and historical explorations of Norse mythology and Danish ballad material provided a rich source of inspiration, influencing themes and motifs. It is my aim to explore the cultural reception and interpretation of these sources. I will do this through analyses of a broad range of text types that encompass translations and adaptations as well as creative approaches. By delving into the intricate interplay between ancient traditions and contemporary concerns surrounding cultural heritage and national identity, the book will uncover the complex dynamics that shaped one important direction within British Gothic literature. The Scandinavian element in the 'literature of terror' has long deserved focused attention.

Chapter 1

NORSE GOTHIC

This chapter will analyse how translations and adaptations of primarily medieval Icelandic texts created a new archive of terror writing. The English versions were not only included in books of history or philology but also printed as literary pieces to appeal to a wider audience. The translations introduced the age to a new aesthetics significantly different from classical and neoclassical models. Beyond stylistic innovation, I will propose that the category of the sublime in Icelandic texts held a poignant cultural importance. Therefore, the chapter will trace the growing interest in Norse literary tradition to a juncture in British history when the need to establish a cultural lineage became crucial.

Norse poetry was believed to offer insights into the beliefs and values of the Germanic ancestors because Icelandic texts were believed to mirror the mindsets of pre-Christian Anglo-Saxons. This chapter argues that the Norse examples, in the view of eighteenth-century writers, revealed a style of composition that embodied a fearlessness in confronting deeply terrifying aspects of the universe. The heroic nature that was linked with the Germanic forefathers was a concept widely celebrated. Hence, the idea that heroism was found in their poetic remains was eagerly embraced by writers.

The first part of the chapter will examine how Icelandic texts were co-opted as representative of Anglo-Saxon traditions, providing England with a long literary pedigree partly motivated by rivalry with the popular Ossian poetry, representing Britain's Celtic heritage. The second part of the chapter will discuss how Norse poetry was reinterpreted and reimagined to highlight the frightening and unsettling elements present in the original verses.

The Influence of Norse Tradition on Britain's Cultural Landscape

The appreciation of Norse tradition did not come about as a result of a single event or influence. It was the outcome of several converging cultural formations in the eighteenth century. However, if one is to define a significant catalyst, it would be the Genevan scholar Paul-Henri Mallet's Francophone works on wider Nordic history and poetry (published 1755–56). Especially pertinent to this chapter are his selected translations from the Poetic Edda (the collection of mythological poems written down in Iceland during the thirteenth century, but of older date) and Skaldic poetry (Norse court poetry developed between the ninth and the thirteenth centuries). These works were well-received across Europe. In Britain, the literary antiquarian Thomas Percy published an abbreviation of these works under the title *Northern Antiquities* in 1780. The title page states that the content was also valid for 'our own Saxon ancestors', even though Mallet only mentions the Anglo-Saxons in passing.[1] Percy made clear (as Mallet had not) that the studies did not address Celtic culture but specifically 'Gothic', or the Germanic heritage of Europe. In fact, the term 'Gothic' had been associated specifically with Norse tradition for a long time, as is apparent in the title of the Danish historian Ole Worm's Latin treatise *Runir* [in runic script] *seu Danica literatura antiquissima, vulgo Gothica dicta luci reddita* [Runes: or the Most Ancient Danish Letters, Popularly Called Gothic, Brought to Light] (1636, rev. 1651), which was indeed one of Mallet's main sources.

Mallet's descriptions and translations of Norse tradition provided a repository of sublime images. There is the image of the war god Odin, the 'terrible Deity who took such pleasure in shedding the blood of men' on the battlefield.[2] But one could also learn about the human sacrifices, journeys to the underworld, female diviners and the end of the world when 'the great Ash tree shakes its branches, heaven and earth are full of horror and affright'.[3] In addition, Mallet's translation of *Rúnatal* (Odin's 'Rune Song' from the Poetic Edda) contains 'Magic Poetry' with the ability to raise the dead.[4]

Initially, British interest in Norse tradition was mainly from literary historians and antiquarians. Thomas Warton saw it as an essential prerequisite for understanding literary development in his *The History of English Poetry* (1774). Warton would trace English poetry not only to its Norse origins but also further back to Eastern sources, seizing on the theory that Odinic mythology was imported from Asia to Scandinavia through ancient migration

---

1 Paul-Henri Mallet, *Northern Antiquities: or, a Description of the Manners, Customs, Religion and Laws of the Ancient Danes, and Other Northern Nations; Including Those of Our Own Saxon Ancestors*, trans. Thomas Percy, 2 vols (London: T. Carnan and Co., 1770).
2 Ibid., 1:87.
3 Ibid., 1:115.
4 Ibid., 2:220.

(a theory elaborated initially by the Icelandic historian Snorri Sturluson around the turn of the thirteenth century).[5] Like Mallet, Warton believed that the climate was a significant factor in influencing the mentalities of various peoples. He claimed that Eastern influences became combined with a northern disposition for gloom. Hence, the supernatural inclinations of Eastern poetry attained 'a darker shade and a more savage complexion' on account of 'the formidable objects of nature to which they became familiarised in those northern solitudes, the piny precipices, the frozen mountains, and the gloomy forests', acting on the Scandinavians' imaginations to add 'a tincture of horror to their imagery'.[6]

An example of the horror that the Norse tradition exhibited can be found in the Icelandic poem known as the eulogium of King Haakon (*Hákonarmál*), a funeral celebration of the Norwegian king who fell in 959. Mallet had translated the poem into French as an example of ancient Scandinavian poetry, but it was also translated into German by J. G. Herder in his collection of *Volkslieder* [Folk ballads] (1778–79). This is a collection of various ethnic and national poetic traditions he believed reflected the *Volksgeist* [folk-soul] of nations. The song reads as a compendium of the dark tropes that came to be associated with Norse tradition. The text describes the carnage Haakon causes on the battlefield and how enemy wounds flow with blood. The spinners of fate invite him to their banquet so that he ('still all besprinkled and running down with blood') arrives in Valhalla, where he meets Odin and exclaims: 'How severe and terrible doth this God appear to me!'[7] The poem exemplified what one may call a dark battlefield Gothic, characterised by explicit gore and a supernatural framework. Eighteenth-century readers increasingly admired sublime images. Thus, when the poem was printed in *The Massachusetts Magazine* in 1791, it was precisely praised for its 'sublimity of fiction'.[8] However, the stark imagery in pieces like this exceeded what some thought suited classical aesthetic categories. As one observer commented: 'The imagery supplied by the Scandinavian poetry is oftentimes more horrible than sublime'.[9] The literary horror of the eulogium of King Haakon

---

5 For the Odin migration theory, see Robert W. Rix, 'Oriental Odin: Tracing the East in Northern Culture and Literature', *History of European Ideas* 36, no. 1 (2010): 47–60.

6 Thomas Warton, 'On the Origin of Romantic Fiction in Europe', in *The History of English Poetry, from the Close of the Eleventh to the Commencement of the Eighteenth Century*, vol. 1 (London: J. Dodsley et al., 1774), [30].

7 Mallet, *Northern Antiquities*, 2:242.

8 'Eulogium of Hacon, King of Norway', *The Massachusetts Magazine* (September 1791): 565.

9 'Domestic Literature of the Year 1784', *The New Annual Register* (1784): 210–76 (270).

was confirmed when it was turned into a Gothic ballad by Matthew Lewis in his *Tales of Wonder* (1801).

It was remarkable to modern readers that Norse warriors welcomed death on the battlefield, believing it would lead to eternal happiness in Valhalla. This belief became a central tenet in writing about the ancestors. The Danish antiquarian Thomas Bartholin had printed parts of the Eulogium in his thesis *Antiqvitatum Danicarum de causis contempta a Danis adhuc gentilibus mortis* [Danish antiquities on the reasons for the death defiance of the heathen Danes] (1689), which was an important book for the reception as it contained parallel Icelandic and Latin texts.[10] Bartholin's overarching theory was that the ancient Scandinavians showed unparalleled bravery in battle because of their superstitious beliefs. Bartholin's book became a standard reference work and introduced the idea of Norse culture as connected to superstition, most concretely in relation to the belief that a heroic death on the battlefield would earn one a place in Valhalla. However, there were also other links between Norse martial prowess and supernatural beliefs, which will be examined in this chapter.

In the British context, what stimulated the interest in the Norse tradition was another 'Northern' tradition: the Scottish antiquarian James Macpherson's purported translations of Gaelic oral verses, allegedly preserved in the Scottish Highlands from third-century bard Ossian. *Fragments of Ancient Poetry* (1760) and the subsequent publications of Ossianic epics became a sensation around Europe. The Ossian poems sparked a fierce controversy in Britain about Scottish history, literature and identity. This has been documented by Colin Kidd, who also emphasises how Macpherson catalysed a remapping of Britain's ethnic heritage as divided sharply between Celtic and Gothic ancestral lines.[11] If the Ossian tales of brave fighters in Caledonia rekindled memories of Scottish liberty, what Macpherson's intentions were are not clear. Recent evaluations have questioned whether Macpherson's publications can be seen as a reactionary response to the Jacobite rebellion of 1745. Juliet Shields, for example, points out that Macpherson's literary ambitions extended beyond the Scottish Highlands and had a strong financial interest in not alienating the wider Lowland and English readership.[12] Nonetheless, the success of the Gaelic tradition that Ossian represented rendered legible the tensions

---

10 Thomas Bartholin, *Antiqvitatum Danicarum de causis contempta a Danis adhuc gentilibus mortis* (Hafnia: J. Phil. Bockenhoffer, 1689). The poem is printed on pp. 522–28.

11 Colin Kidd, *Subverting Scotland's Past: Scottish Whig Historians and the Creation of an Anglo-British Identity 1689–1830* (Cambridge: Cambridge University Press, 1993).

12 Juliette Shields, *Sentimental Literature and Anglo-Scottish Identity, 1745–1820* (Cambridge: Cambridge University Press, 2010), 45.

between England and Scotland. It was soon suspected that the poems were fraudulent, and English detractors accused supporters of Ossian of carrying the flag for Highland nationalism. As Samuel Johnson expressed it, the Ossian sensation was 'another proof of Scotch conspiracy in national falsehood'.[13] This cultural debate resulted in English poetic tradition being traced as 'Gothic', and Norse specimens were considered the oldest extant archive of this legacy recorded in writing. The extent to which the interest in ethnic Gothic is also reflected in the literary Gothic has been probed by Carol Margaret Davison, who notes that Horace Walpole was not only a fierce critic of Macpherson's Ossian but also used 'the ethnographically loaded' subtitle 'A Gothic Story' for his 1765 edition of *The Castle of Otranto*, signalling his participation in the vexed cultural competition between Germanic and Celtic traditions.[14] Walpole references Shakespeare as his main inspiration for the book, and Shakespeare's use of ghosts and folkloric material could be seen as having kept Germanic tradition alive. Samuel Johnson, for example, wrote about *A Midsummer Night's Dream* in 1765 that the play contains 'the Gothick mythology of fairies'.[15]

The cultural divide did not align with national borders. The lowland Scots were part of the Gothic/Scandinavian heritage, while the Celtic tradition was culturally confined to the Highlands. The most famous Scottish writer, Walter Scott, sets both *The Lady of the Lake* (1810) and *The Lord of the Isles* (1815) in the Highlands without mentioning the Ossian tradition. Instead, he took an interest in the Germanic and especially Scandinavian tradition of supernaturalism. In his review of the 1805 Laing edition of the Ossian publications, Scott accuses Macpherson of introducing a surfeit of eighteenth-century 'sentimental effusion', which cannot have been present in the original Gaelic material.[16] If sentimentalism was clearly the selling point of the Ossian publications, Scott saw Macpherson failing to implement an effective supernatural element. Since Macpherson found nothing he could use in the oral material and dared not invent a mythology of his own for fear of being

---

13 Cited in Thomas M. Curley, *Samuel Johnson, the Ossian Fraud, and the Celtic Revival in Great Britain and Ireland* (Cambridge: Cambridge University Press, 2009), 289.

14 Carol Margaret Davison, 'The Politics and Poetics of the "Scottish Gothic" from Ossian to Otranto and Beyond', in *Scottish Gothic: An Edinburgh Companion*, ed. Carol Margaret Davison and Monica Germanà (Edinburgh: Edinburgh University Press, 2017), 28–41 (30).

15 Samuel Johnson, 'Preface to *The Plays of William Shakespeare*' (1765), in *Selected Works*, ed. Robert DeMaria, Jr., Stephen Fix, and Howard D. Weinbrot (New Haven: Yale University Press, 2021), 425–62 (433).

16 Walter Scott, review of *Report of the Highland Society of Scotland* [...] *and the Poems of Ossian* [...] *Works of James Macpherson*, in *Edinburgh Review* 6, no. 12 (July 1805): 446.

exposed as a fraud, he was forced to confine himself to 'the vulgar superstition concerning the spirits the departed common to the Highlanders'.[17] Hence, what is found in the poems is the 'useless appearance of [] impotent phantoms' causing 'contempt' rather than 'fear or reverence'.[18]

Indeed, Scotland had an alternative ethno-Gothic tradition through Danish occupation and raids. This was believed to have nourished the ballads and folklore. In his *Lady of the Lake* (1810), set in the Trossachs region of the Highlands, Scott showed his interest in Danish ballads – including two specimens, one of them being the ghost story 'Ghaist's Warning'.[19] Already in 1749, the English poet William Collins wrote 'An Ode on the Popular Superstitions of the Highlands of Scotland, Considered as the Subject of Poetry'. The poem is addressed to John Home, a Scottish playwright who attempted to stage his plays in London, summoning him back to Scotland to find inspiration in the 'strange lays', 'hideous spells', 'gliding ghosts' and 'phantom train' in the Highland tradition.[20] Collins calls attention to the fount of imagination that modern writers may take after

> Old Runic bards shall seem to rise around,
> With uncouth lyres, in many-coloured vest,
> Their matted hair with boughs fantastic crowned[21]

The lines were only published posthumously, in 1788, when the Gothic appropriation of Norse material was well underway. Appearing in numerous periodicals that year, Collins contributed to the cultural force of writers aiming to renew the repertoire of poetic composition by looking back to ethnic traditions.

The Norse tradition was actively promoted as a counterpoint to Macpherson's successful publications. One example is Thomas Percy's anthology *Five Pieces of Runic Poetry Translated from the Islandic Language* (1763), which was, as he explains, a direct reaction to 'the success of the ERSE fragments [i.e. Macpherson's *Fragments of Ancient Poetry*]'.[22] The Skaldic

---

17 Ibid., 447.
18 Ibid.
19 Walter Scott, *The Lady of the Lake: A Poem* (Edinburgh: John Ballantyne, 1810), 367–80.
20 William Collins, 'An Ode on the Popular Superstitions of the Highlands of Scotland, Considered as the Subject of Poetry', *Transactions of the Royal Society of Edinburgh* 1 (Edinburgh: J. Dickson, 1788), 63–75 (68–69).
21 Ibid., 68.
22 Thomas Percy, *Five Pieces of Runic Poetry Translated from the Islandic Language* (London: R. and J. Dodsley, 1763), [vi].

poems from the medieval North depict the violent aspects of the tradition, despite Percy's attempts to emphasise their softer facets in his notes. While some might perceive barbarism in the Norsemen's belligerent attitudes, the bravery and zeal of the Norse warriors could be viewed as a desirable ethnic-cultural trait. John Pinkerton, a Scottish antiquarian and early advocate of Gothic/Germanic supremacy, believed that Gothic poetry expressed wholesome courage, while the sentimentalism in Ossian was a sign of cultural failure:

> The Celtic poetry, as that of a weak and dispirited people might be expected to be, is almost wholly melancholic in a supreme degree. All the mock Ossian is full of misery and death. The Gothic poetry is the exact reverse of this, being replete with that warm alacrity of mind cheerful courage and quick wisdom which attend superior talents.[23]

Pinkerton's ethnically biased preference for Gothic (i.e. Norse) poetry was echoed by the reviewer of his book in the *Critical Review*: 'We may indeed allow that the verse of the Goths is more violent animated and fierce than that of the Celts'; indeed, Norse poems are 'replete with warm alacrity of mind chearful courage and quick wisdom [...] with bold enterprize, spirited horror, and fierce revenge'.[24]

A similar negative evaluation in favour of the Gothic-Germanic tradition is found in J. G. Herder's philosophical reflection on using Norse mythology for the renewal of German poetry, *Iduna, oder der Apfel der Verjüngung* [Iduna, or the apple of rejuvenation] (1796). In this text, one of the speakers, Alfred, slights the poetry of Ossian for its 'soft, sad feelings', while he praises the Nordic people as 'the liberators of a world subjugated by a cowardly, lavish servitude'.[25] Reflecting on the tenor of these statements, it is worth speculating on the connection between Norse poetry and its regular adaptation as terror literature in eighteenth- and nineteenth-century publications. I will propose that what may be called 'Norse Gothic' was promoted partly through rivalry with the overt sentimentalism of the Ossian poems. The Germanic forefathers'

---

23 John Pinkerton, *An Enquiry into the History of Scotland: Preceding the Reign of Malcolm III*, new ed. (Edinburgh: Bell et al. 1814), 388–89.
24 Review of *An Enquiry into the History of Scotland*, in *The Critical Review* (July 1790): 21.
25 J. G. Herder, 'Iduna, oder der Apfel der Verjüngung', *Die Horen: Eine Monatsschrift* 5 (1796): 1–28 (20), 'Der Gale sang weiche, traurige Empfindungen; der Normann sang Thaten [...] Die ältesten Nordländer waren die Befreier der Welt, die von einer feigen, üppigen Knechtschaft unterjocht war'.

unsentimental and dark aesthetics were interpreted as a cultural strength. The horrific and unsettling images of the past showcased the ancestors' fearlessness and indomitable spirit. From this perspective, the poet's engagement with the supernatural or the numinous, as seen in the eulogium of Haakon, was made to stand as the epitome of Germanic audaciousness. In other words, the Skalds showed their mettle in their imaginative encounters with death and its horrible emissaries.

Walter Scott reflects on these ideas in his poem *The Lay of the Last Minstrel* (1805), where the appearance of the warrior Harold from the Norse-occupied Orkney Islands allows Scott to make several references to Scandinavian tradition in his scholarly notes. For example, he mentions that the Norse ancestors 'held nothing more worthy of their valour than to encounter supernatural beings'.[26] If facing supernatural entities was considered a heroic trait in the past, some of this heroism may rub off on the modern writer, for whom it was a distinctive challenge to represent the ghostly with appropriately sublime and evocative imagery. In 'Imitations of the Ancient Ballads' (1821), Scott praises German poets who draw inspiration from Northern superstition (such as Goethe, Schiller and Bürger), extolling their virtues as 'a race of poets who had the [...] lofty ambition to spurn the flaming boundaries of the universe and investigate the realms of chaos and old night'.[27] The Norse tradition, with its blood-soaked deaths and terrifying pagan deities, was a source of horror that captivated eighteenth-century readers and directly appealed to readers of Gothic literature. In contrast, the overriding melancholic tone in Macpherson's Ossian poems did not sit well with the terror required for Gothic novels. As Dale Townshend notes, the spectral presences in Macpherson's Ossian do not terrorise the living; warriors such as Shilric and Malcolm invite spectres to mourn the tragedy of death with them.[28] Unlike in Gothic literature, as we know it, ghosts are not disruptive forces but become part of living society's positive connection with the past.

It is ironic that Hugh Blair, who wrote against the blood-and-battle aesthetics of Norse poetry, would identify a battle with the spirit of the Norse god Odin (referred to as 'Loda') as a high point of Ossian's poetry.

---

26 Walter Scott, *The Lay of the Last Minstrel: A Poem*, 3rd ed. (London: Longman et al., 1806), 328.

27 Walter Scott, 'Imitations of the Ancient Ballads', in *Minstrelsy of the Scottish Border*, 5 ed., vol. 1 (London: Longman et al. 1821), 42.

28 Dale Townshend, 'Shakespeare, Ossian and the Problem of "Scottish Gothic"', in *Gothic Renaissance: A Reassessment*, ed. Elisabeth Bronfen and Beate Neumeier (Manchester: Manchester University Press, 2014), 218–43, see esp. 232–35.

In the fragment, *Carric-Thura*, the Gaelic hero Fingal engages in combat with the spirit of Odin, who emerges out of a cloud in the Orkneys. Blair asserts that this scene 'must have drawn the attention of everyone' since there 'was no passage more sublime' in its 'most amazing and terrible majesty'.[29] The passage details 'all the terrors of the Scandinavian god; the appearance and the speech of that awful spirit; the wound which he receives, and the shriek which he sends forth'.[30] It is remarkable that Blair picks this passage because it is an uncharacteristically hostile encounter with a ghostly being in the Ossian poems. In contrast, the Norse tradition had several such well-known confrontations between the living and supernatural beings. In the following section, I will delve into the confrontations that became known and recognised as significant hallmarks of Norse poetry in Britain.

Facing the Revenants

One of the most frequently translated poems from the Norse tradition that concretely depicted a confrontation with a ghost was 'The Waking of Angantyr' (*Hervararkviða*), excerpted from the thirteenth-century Saga of Hervǫr and King Heidrek (*Hervarar saga ok Heiðreks.*), translated into Latin in Bartholin's *Antiqvitatum Danicarum*. The Oxford philologist George Hickes provided the first English translation in Volume I of his extensive *Thesaurus* (1703). It was later translated by John Dryden (1716). There were also adaptations by Thomas Percy (1763), Thomas James Mathias (1781) and William Bagshawe Stevens (1775). The poem was deemed suitable as magazine poetry at the end of the eighteenth century (*The Gentlemen's Magazine*, September 1790), and it was printed by both Joseph Sterling (1794) and Matthew Lewis (1801).

The poem concerns Hervǫr (also known as Hervar, Herva or Hervor in English translations), a shield-maiden who has travelled with her fleet to the haunted Danish island of Samsø. She is the only one who dares to go ashore. Hervǫr enters the largest barrow on the island to summon her father, Angantyr, to demand possession of Tyrfing, a magic but cursed sword. The poem is a stand-off between the bold Hervǫr and Angantyr's frightening *draugr* or *haugbui* (animated corpse). At first, Angantyr refuses to yield the sword but finally bends to Hervǫr's heroic insistence. The poem epitomised the bravery of the Norse ancestors, and it was a bravery that would reach its absolute height in the confrontation with a revenant. In a note to

---

29 Blair, *Critical Dissertation*, 39.
30 Ibid.

The Lay of the Last Minstrel (1805), Walter Scott explains that the poem's ghost story reflects ethnonational traits of heroism:

> Indeed, the ghosts of the northern warriors would not suffer their tombs to be plundered, and hence, the mortal heroes had an additional temptation to attempt such adventures. For they held nothing more worthy of their valour than to encounter supernatural beings.[31]

The defiance of death, whether it is in the form of ghosts or one's own demise, is expanded upon in Matthew Lewis' adaptation, 'The Sword of Angantyr', printed in *Tales of Wonder*. Lewis writes in the headnote to the poem that he has 'taken great liberties with it' and that the 'catastrophe' at the end is his 'own invention'.[32] Instead of having the shield maiden walk away victorious from Angantyr's tomb, Lewis' new conclusion has Hervǫr suffer the curse of the magic sword she has pried from her father. Lewis revels in portraying Hervǫr's intense pain of being engulfed by flames (borrowing a literary technique of repeating a single word in immediate succession from Shakespeare and Milton):

> Curses! Curses! oh! what pain!
> How my melting eye-balls glow!
> Curses! curses! through each vein
> How do boiling torrents flow![33]

This tragic ending is inconsistent with the saga from which the poem was originally extracted, as it tells the continued history of Hervǫr and her family over several generations. Lewis' decision to kill off Hervǫr, however, maximises the terror of the scene. At the same time, he adds additional resilience and fearlessness to Hervǫr's character; her last words apostrophise the goddess of the underworld: 'Hela! I obey thy power, / Hela! take thy willing slave'.[34] While one may accuse Lewis of lacking knowledge about (or displaying indifference towards) the original legend of Hervǫr, it is evident that he, with his new ending, had internalised the notion of Norse heroes displaying unwavering bravery in the face of death or eternal punishment.

Framing Gothic literature as part of a cultural formation in Britain, Michael Gamer has argued that invoking the supernatural was a particularly masculine endeavour; its feminine opposite was the controlled realist Gothic fiction of authors like Ann Radcliffe, who would explain away the

---

31 Walter Scott, *The Lay of the Last Minstrel: A Poem* (London: Longman, Hurst, Rees and Orme, 1805), 213.
32 Matthew Lewis, *Tales of Wonder*, 2 vols. (London: J. Bell, 1801), 1:34.
33 Ibid., 1:44.
34 Ibid.

seemingly supernatural as mere illusions or hoaxes.[35] However, the female heroism displayed in the encounter with Angantyr allowed for revision of these gender roles.[36] This was embraced by the poet Anna Seward in her version, 'Herva at the Tomb of Argantyr: A Runic Dialogue' (1796), which she describes as a 'bold Paraphrase' (which also slightly changes the name of the revenant father).[37] Now, Hervǫr not only relies on the toughness of a male warrior but also manipulates the realm of the dead through daring magic:

> ARGANTYR, wake! – to thee I call,
> Hear from thy dark sepulchral hall!
> 'Mid the forest's inmost gloom,
> Thy daughter, circling thrice thy tomb,
> With mystic rites of thrilling power
> Disturbs thee at this midnight hour![38]

Seward's changes to the poem were well received for invoking 'sublime terrour', as the *Analytical Review* described it.[39]

The Norse poem's iconic quality inspired others to find similar examples of confronting ghosts. In 1789, the English poet and antiquarian Richard Hole published a paraphrase of the poem 'The Tomb of Gunnar' (from the late thirteenth-century *Njals Saga*), which Bartholin had printed in his thesis on the death-defiant Scandinavians.[40] The poem concerns the famous warrior Gunnar Hámundarson, who awakens in his tomb with 'dreadful sounds', frightening a shepherd who is walking under the 'moon's uncertain light'.[41] Gunnar's son, Högni, and a friend are summoned, and they approach the tomb, which is hidden by 'darkly-rolling vapours', to discover that Gunnar is singing a song of martial prowess: 'Unmanly flight the brave despise / Conquest of death is the warrior's prize!', which in turn motivates the two tomb intruders to preparing 'a banquet for the wolf' on the battlefield.[42]

---

35 Michael Gamer, *Romanticism and the Gothic: Genre, Reception, and Canon Formation* (Cambridge: Cambridge University Press, 2000), 53.

36 For the appreciation of females in Norse poetry during the period, see Sydney Lines, 'Norse Romanticism: Subversive Female Voices in British Invocations of Nordic Yore', PhD thesis, Arizona State University, 2013.

37 Anna Seward, *Llangollen Vale, with Other Poems* (London: G. Sael, 1796), 22–23.

38 Ibid.

39 Review of Seward, *Llangollen Vale*, in *The Analytical Review* (April 1796): 389.

40 Richard Hole, 'The Tomb of Gunnar. Imitated from an Ancient Islandic Fragment, preserved by Bartholin', *Gentleman's Magazine* (October 1789): 937; Bartholin, *Antiqvitatum Danicarum*, 279–81.

41 Hole, 'The Tomb of Gunnar', 937.

42 Ibid.

While vernacular poetry of the past afforded a privileged insight into the imagination and beliefs of the ancestors unavailable in other sources, the models of bravery contained in the pieces of Norse Gothic also served as a commentary on the present. We may here recall David Punter's observation that the 'code of Gothic' is a simple one in which 'past is encoded in the present or vice versa, but dialectical, past and present intertwined, each distorting each other'.[43] It is interesting to note that Richard Hole's translation of 'The Tomb of Gunnar' as well as an anonymous version of 'The Waking of Angantyr' were reprinted in *Poems Chiefly by Gentlemen of Devonshire and Cornwall* (1792), as it suggests the poems about taking a warrior code from the heroes of the past could be recontextualised for an age when Britain was at war with France. At least, the war is directly reflected in one of the poems in the collection: Edward Drewe's 'The Rapt Bard'. The verses include the warning: 'Hostile nations seek our shore; / Lo! I mark their dread advance, / See the fleet of faithless France!'[44] Was such a constellation of old and new models of bravery intentional? In this respect, we may heed Dafydd Moore's assessment of ancient heroic texts revived in times of unrest and war: 'the Gothic past was victim to political overdetermination'.[45] Certainly, Hole's dedication to patriotic discourse cannot be doubted. He had earlier published the verse romance *Arthur, or the Northern Enchantment. In Seven Books* (1789), which focuses on a British heroic king beset by supernatural adversaries, for which Hole provides numerous notes on Scandinavian supernaturalism.

Norse Odes

Having explored representations of encounters with supernatural beings in relation to the translation of Norse poetry, this next section will focus on the two preeminent translations that captured the imagination of eighteenth-century readers and writers, introducing them to Norse tradition as an archive brimming with sublime imagery. The poems in question are Thomas Gray's 'The Fatal Sisters. An Ode', the original source of which is known as *Darraðarljoð* and derives from chapter 157 of *Njáls saga* (thirteenth century), and 'The Descent of Odin', a translation of the poem *Baldrs draumar* (Balder's Dreams) or *Vegtamskviða* (The Lay of the Wayfarer) from

---

43 David Punter, *The Literature of Terror: History of Gothic Fiction from 1765 to the Present Day* (London: Longman, 1980), 418.

44 *Poems Chiefly by Gentlemen of Devonshire and Cornwall*, 2 vols. ed. Richard Polwhele (Bath: T. Cadell, 1792), 1:32.

45 Dafydd Moore, 'Patriotism, Politeness, and National Identity in the South West of England in the Late Eighteenth Century', *ELH* 76, no. 3 (2009): 739–62 (750).

the Poetic Edda. Gray had no knowledge of Icelandic and worked from Latin translations by seventeenth-century scholars Thormod Torfæus and Thomas Bartholin.

Gray produced the translations in 1761, but they were not published until the bookseller Robert Dodsley included them in the 1768 edition of Gray's Poems. In the short 'Advertisement', Gray explains that the odes were originally intended for a '*History of English Poetry*', in the introduction to which he meant to include 'specimens of the Style that reigned in ancient times among the neighbouring nations, or those who had subdued the greater part of this Island, and were our Progenitors'.[46] However, the plans for this literary history were dropped. According to Margaret Omberg, Macpherson's publication of Ossian poems, the first instalment of which came out in 1760, greatly influenced Gray and made him want to include an equivalent tradition for Britain's Germanic tradition.[47] Kelsey Jackson Williams concurs, asserting that 'it would be perverse to read Gray's 1761 translations from the Old Norse as anything other than a reaction to Macpherson's publications'.[48] The poems can thus be seen as another intervention in the Gaelic-Germanic culture war discussed above. The literary critic Nathan Drake, who encouraged writers to take inspiration from Norse tradition, praised in the 1797 edition of *Literary Hours* 'the thrilling horror of Gray's celebrated odes [...] which first opened to English poetry a mine of the most wild yet terrific mythology', while he states that the 'features of the Celtic [Ossianic tradition] are certainly not of so striking a form', but nonetheless of great worth.[49]

In considering a literary history of English verse, Gray likely chose to include 'The Fatal Sisters' because of its link to Scotland. The background for the poem is the history of the Norse Earl of the Orkney Islands, who sent a fleet of ships into Ireland, resulting in the Battle of Clontarff, near Dublin in 1014. On the day of the battle, a native of Caithness, Scotland, peeks through a gap in a hill and sees gigantic female figures who are employed about a loom. These females are the Norns, female deities in Norse mythology responsible for shaping the destinies of humans. In the cave, they are occupied with weaving

46 *Poems by Mr. Gray, A New Edition* (London: J. Dodsley, 1768), 75.
47 Margaret Omberg, *Scandinavian Themes in English Poetry, 1760–1800* (Uppsala: Uppsala University, 1976), 26.
48 Kelsey Jackson Williams, 'Thomas Gray and the Goths: Philology, Poetry, and the Uses of the Norse Past in Eighteenth-Century England', *Review of English Studies* 65 (2014): 694–710 (707).
49 Nathan Drake, *Literary Hours: or, Sketches Critical and Narrative* (London: T. Cadell and W. Davies, 1798), 380.

the destinies of the warriors in the impending battle. Their cloth is the fate of combatants, which is placed on a terrible loom made up of human corpses:

> Grisly texture grow,
> ('Tis of human entrails made,)
> And the weights that play below,
> Each a gasping Warriour's head.
> Shafts for shuttles, dipt in gore,
> Shoot the trembling cords along.[50]

It is worth noting that Gray is not attempting to produce a philologically accurate translation; it is a rather free paraphrase of the original, with some of the lines bearing little or no relationship to the Latin source text. Even where he follows the original, Gray often adds adjectives, such as 'griesly', 'gasping' and 'trembling', to amplify the terror of the piece. Even if the translation was conceived as a contribution to the planned scholarly history of English poetry, it is evident that Gray modifies the lines with the intention of captivating and engaging readers.

Yet Gray was keenly aware of the poem's cultural resonance in a British context. An entry dated 1761 in the third volume of Gray's Commonplace Books (now in Pembroke College, Cambridge Library), under the heading 'Gothi', refers to the Norse poem as 'The Song of the Weird Sisters, or Valkyries'.[51] That Shakespeare's three witches ('Weird Sisters') derived from Norse mythology was a theory also proposed by the critic William Warburton. In his edition of *Macbeth* (first published 1747), a note explains that the three witches were a version of 'the *Fates* of the northern nations; the three hand-maids of *Odin*'.[52] The underpinning idea here is that Shakespeare drew on a part of Scottish folklore that contained corrupted remnants of the Norse religion, left there by Scandinavians who had settled the nearby Orkneys.

The Orkney and Shetland Islands had been under Norse control since the ninth century and only officially became Scottish territory in 1472. The impact of Norse culture on the Islands is a central theme in Walter Scott's Waverley novel *The Pirate* (1822), to which I will return in Chapter 4. What is important here is that the action takes place on an island of the remote Shetlands at the end of the seventeenth century. The story has a romantic plot

---

50 Gray, *Poems*, 80.
51 Thomas Gray, Commonplace Book, vol. 3, p. 56v, Cambridge University Digital Library, https://cudl.lib.cam.ac.uk/view/MS-PEMBROKE-GRA-00001-00003/1.
52 *The Plays of William Shakespeare*, vol. 6, ed. William Warburton (London: J. and P. Knapto et al., 1747), 338.

but centrally explores cultural change and the passing of an old way of life for the making of a new Britain. For the novel's setting, Scott recalled two weeks spent in Orkney and Shetland in 1814 with the Commissioners for the Northern Lighthouse Service. In a note to later editions of the novel, Scott references a visit to North Ronaldsay, Orkney's most northerly island, where a clergyman gave information about Norn, a now-extinct North Germanic language, spoken in these parts. The clergyman could remember when Gray's 'The Fatal Sisters' first reached the remote island, and he read it to some of the old people there. After they had heard a few verses, they interrupted him and explained 'that they knew the song well in the Norse language' and that '[t]hey called it The Magicians or the Enchantresses'.[53] If Macpherson claimed to have found an oral Gaelic tradition preserved in the Highlands, Scott here makes a competitive claim for Norse tradition in the Orkneys. Here, we can discern some of the fault lines underlying larger ethno-cultural discussions unfolding nationally in the early nineteenth century. Scott's example demonstrates how the discovery of Norse poetry could be negotiated with indigenous history. Rather than viewing Norse heritage as a foreign import, Scott saw it as part of the rich national character shaped by a long history of occupations and literary influences. His description of the resilient Scandinavian seam reinforced the notion that Scottish identity was partly rooted in a Nordic tradition. It should here be remembered that the impetus to look for historical roots was that they were believed to explain both the mentality and aesthetic orientation of the present. Thus, such remembrances of tradition connected Scotland with its Gothic ancestry.

Gray's 'The Fatal Sisters' had a long-lasting influence on pre-Romantic- and Romantic-period writers who sought an alternative to neoclassical aesthetics. Choosing a subject from British history, Richard Hole's *Arthur, or, The Northern Enchantments* (1789), which was mentioned above, includes numerous references to witches. Early in the poem, the Weird Sisters appear, described as '[t]hree female forms' performing a 'mystic rite' as they 'rouz'd th'infernal powers'.[54] In the preface, Hole clarifies that he is thinking of the three Norns of Norse mythology but has accommodated the representation to be more like the lowlier witches in *Macbeth* to fit the representation to 'our British system of Dæmonology'.[55] Hole shows the intertwining of antiquarian study of the Norse influence on British history and his literary interest in exploiting Norse supernatural elements for their

53 Walter Scott, *The Pirate, Waverley Novels* vol. 24 (Edinburgh: Robert Cadell, 1831), 29.
54 Richard Hole, *Arthur, or, The Northern Enchantments* (London: G. G. J. and J. Robinson: 1789), 7.
55 Ibid., ii–viii.

literary effects. In the Preface, Hole tells the reader that he has chosen to mine 'the old Gothic fables' for inspiration because they are 'less hackneyed' than classical tradition and 'afford more materials for the writer's imagination'.[56]

Gray was commended by contemporaries for his bravery in having, like the inhabitant of Caithness in the poem, gazed upon such horrifying Norse sceneries. In one of his poetic epistles, the poet William Hayley commended Gray for being 'solicitous to pierce / The dark and distant source of modern Verse, / By strings untried first taught his English Lyre / To reach the Gothic Harp's terrific fire'.[57] If the Norse tradition commanded attention from an ethno-national perspective, the appreciation of it was also helped by shifting aesthetic preferences. From the late eighteenth century, interest in the vernacular past was added to a continuing reverence for the classical tradition. Bishop Richard Hurd's *Letters on Chivalry and Romance* (1762) is often viewed as a harbinger of this change. Hurd contends that vernacular superstition provides a more potent outlet for literary imagination than what is offered by classical writers. Thus, he commends Milton for 'conjuring up [...] the Gothic language and ideas' when he wants to 'paint the horrors of that night'.[58] In fact, 'modern bards' may also benefit from creating a 'more sublime, more terrible' scene than that of the 'classic fablers' by taking advantage of vernacular superstitions, because they will become 'more poetical for being Gothic'.[59] The appearance of Norse terrors in both English translation and new composition can be understood as a result of writers seeking an alternative to the overused neoclassical conventions. At the same time, they could claim to be reviving a traditional mode of composition that respected the past.

Mythological Terrors

Having explored the depiction of the three ominous figures who control the thread of human destiny in 'The Fatal Sister', I will now consider Gray's second ode, 'The Descent of Odin', which elevates the themes of destiny to a cosmic scale by foreshadowing the ending of the world. This poem also had a foundational influence on British literature in the eighteenth century. The poem concerns the tragic circumstances of the god Baldr's death. Gray omits the first lines of the original poem, describing the gods holding

---

56 Ibid. iv.
57 William Hayley, *An Essay on Epic Poetry, in Five Epistles* (Dublin: S. Price et al., 1782), 39–40.
58 Richard Hurd, *Letters on Chivalry and Romance* (London: A. Millar, W. Thurlbourn, and J. Woodyer, 1762), 52.
59 Ibid., 54–55.

a council about the situation so that the translation begins *in medias res* with Odin donning a disguise to enter the underworld. Odin uses a magic incantation to awaken a *völva* (seeress) from her deathlike state to learn about Baldr's death, foretold in a dream. However, Odin's identity is accidentally revealed, and the seeress bids him leave. Mallet had been clearly fascinated with how Norse diviners would regularly disturb the dead to know about the future; and that even the bards 'boasted a power of disturbing the repose of the dead, and of dragging them out of their gloomy abodes, by force of certain songs which they knew how to compose'.[60] Gray's depiction of the waking of the *völva* achieved an iconic status in English literature. This is to the extent that his translation was echoed many years later in Charles Maturin's Gothic novel *Melmoth the Wanderer* (1820). In the scene where the young Dublin student, John, visits his dying uncle's house, he is greeted by dogs that have 'eyes that glow and fangs that grin'.[61] These lines are taken from Gray's description of the Dog of Darkness that Odin encounters when he descends to the Norse Hel.

In the conclusion of 'The Descent of Odin', there are allusions to *Ragnarök*, when 'substantial Night / Has reaffum'd her ancient right' and 'the fabric of the world will be 'wrapp'd in flames'.[62] These images inspired other writers to translate these parts of the Edda. The poet and critic Thomas James Mathias acknowledges Gray's influence in the title of his collection *Runic Odes: Imitated from the Norse Tongue in the Manner of Mr. Gray* (1781, new editions in 1790 and 1806). Mathias produces two poems about the end of the world: 'Twilight of the Gods' and 'The Renovation of the World'. Both are translations from the Edda (based on Bartholin's Latin versions), presenting the reader with dark and foreboding imagery steeped in ancient legends and prophecies. 'The Twilight of the Gods' warns of a future cataclysm when 'Monstrous female forms advance [...] all from Hela's dark abode'; one must 'Mark the murderous monster stalk' (the unleashed Fenris wolf); and Odin will 'creep to the mansion cold' as a metaphor of his death.[63] Mathias' versions are far from philologically accurate, but neither is this the purpose. His aim is to produce a new type of reading matter for the eighteenth-century book market. When choosing epithets such as monstrous and murderous, he transmutes what can be considered Gothic terror by replacing dark castles with the superior darkness of Hela's abode.

---

60 Mallet, *Northern Antiquities*, 1:147.
61 Charles Maturin, *Melmoth the Wanderer* (Oxford: Oxford University Press, 1998), 10.
62 Gray, *Poems*, 107.
63 Thomas James Mathias, *Runic Odes: Imitated from the Norse Tongue in the Manner of Mr. Gray* (London: T. Payne, 1781), 5–6.

The transition between Norse mythology and the strange magic rites that would later characterise Gothic fiction can be seen in the original composition entitled 'An Incantation Founded on the Northern Mythology', which Mathias added to his collection. The poem is spoken by the sorcerer Thorbiorga, who performs 'magic's secret rite' by calling the 'all and each of hell's grim host, / Howling demon, tortur'd ghost' to hear 'each spell and potent word'.[64] This takes place in a setting when 'midnight torches gleam' as 'Rivals of the Moon's pale beam [...] Some moss-grown ruin silvering o'er'.[65]

The Irish poet and antiquary Joseph Sterling produced a version of 'The Twilight of the Gods' in his *Poems* (1782, 2nd ed. 1789). The first lines are indicative of the sublime and awe-inspiring images that he evidently takes pleasure in rendering for an English-speaking audience:

The dusky moon is streak'd with blood,
The demons of the tempest roar;
A deluge swells the mountain flood,
The clouds descend in streams of gore:
From the dark mansions of the north

Sterling prefaces this poem and the whole section entitled 'Odes from the Icelandic' with a short 'Dissertation', in which he calls Gray 'his guide' on this literary exploration of Norse poetry.[66] The apocalyptic imagery and symbolism found in Norse tradition, which Gray had first brought to literary attention, provided a powerful backdrop for exploring themes of mortality and the fragility of civilisation. With such pieces, we approach what Gary Richard Thompson, in a classic formulation, locates as a regular mode for Gothic writers who would turn to 'terror and horror' in an effort 'to express a complex vision of the existential agony confronting man since the Age of Faith'.[67]

The aesthetic of Norse terror was taken up by writers who sought to tap into a rediscovered vernacular mode of composition at the end of the eighteenth century. One example is the poet Frank Sayers, who published *Dramatic Sketches of the Ancient Northern Mythology* in 1790. The central piece of the collection is the drama *The Descent of Frea*, which is inspired by tales from the Edda about the death of the god Baldr and the descent to the underworld,

---

64 Ibid., 27–28.
65 Ibid., 28.
66 Joseph Sterling, *Poems* (London: G. G. J. & J. Robinson, 1789), 146.
67 Gary Richard Thompson, *The Gothic Imagination: Essays in Dark Romanticism* (Washington: Washington State University, 1974), 5.

here described as a 'land of horror! where eternal Frost / Has built his icy throne and dims the air'.[68] In the preface, Sayers presents his work as part of a longstanding tradition of vernacular writing, utilising 'the superstitions and mythologies which have contributed at different periods to decorate the poetry of England' and praises Gray for having activated this 'splendid and sublime religion of our Northern ancestors' for eighteenth-century writers.[69]

Norse mythological imagination was harnessed in the following years. An example is Joseph Cottle's *Alfred* (1800), which focuses on a Danish ninth-century invasion. The first Book of the poem focuses on Ivar (the son of Ragnar Lodbrog) and his encounter with a witch, who is referred to as the 'great Fatal-Sister' to know his father's fate and his own when undertaking his invasion of England.[70] Ivar also seeks out Hela in the underworld to learn the outcome of his planned invasion of England. The vividly described journey into the earth replaces the conventional dark castle corridors of Gothic narratives. Like in Gray's 'The Descent of Odin', the ruler of the underworld must be woken from her death-like state. Cottle clearly makes the most of this scene. Ivar looks aghast at a 'Coffin, black' with the sorceress lying in 'her narrow bed [...] with death-like sleep', until she is stirred to life and stands up with 'venom'd drops distill'd / Upon her bare head from the craggy roof / Where countless reptiles hung'.[71]

The Norse-inspired Book I is stylistically at variance with the rest of the poem. In the preface, Cottle apologises for his choice but excuses it on the grounds that a modern poet may find a 'peculiar scope to the imagination' in 'the wildness of the Gothic superstitions'.[72] However, unleashing the imaginative potential of Norse mythology comes at a price, as the sublime characters and concepts in Book I are weighed down by long explanatory notes, needed as an extra provision for the system of superstition to be understood. The same issue faced William Beckford, whose Eastern tale, usually known as *Vathek* (1786), is accompanied by extensive notes 'Critical and Explanatory' by his collaborator Samuel Henley, taking up almost a third of the volume.[73]

---

68 Frank Sayers, *Dramatic Sketches of the Ancient Northern Mythology* (London: Joseph Johnson, 1790), 1.

69 Ibid., iii.

70 Joseph Cottle, *Alfred, an Epic Poem, in Twenty-Four Books*, 2nd ed (London: Longman and Rees, 1800), 10.

71 Ibid., 21–23.

72 Ibid., iv.

73 William Beckford, *An Arabian Tale: From an unpublished manuscript with notes critical and explanatory* (London: J. Johnson, 1786).

Norse and Native: A Better Gothic?

Despite the difficulty of overcoming the obscurity of Norse references and making the tradition relevant to the modern age, it was nonetheless what was attempted. Therefore, it is useful to consider briefly the role Norse terror came to play in the politicised British literary system of Gothic productions. For this, we may return to Mathias' *Runic Odes*. Mathias' promotion of Norse terror as a new avenue of literary pursuit is interesting since he is primarily known for his later anti-Jacobin stance against the Gothic, especially Matthew Lewis' *The Monk* (first published 1796), which he pronounced 'an object of moral and national reprehension' in the fourth part of the expansive satire *The Pursuits of Literature* (published on 19 July of 1797).[74] According to Mathias, the fad for the Gothic had weakened the British national spirit and flooded the land with sensational literature of little value:

> Have Gallic arms and unrelenting war
> Borne all her trophies from Britannia far?
> Shall nought but ghosts and trinkets be display'd,
> Since Walpole play'd the virtuoso's trade.[75]

Another strand in Mathias' nationalist culture politics was his 'Europhobia', a term I borrow from Peter Mortensen, manifesting itself in a scepticism of foreign literature.[76] The cultivation of a native literary tradition is also found in the foreword to *The Castle of Otranto*, where Walpole situates his own extravagant production within a national framework that explicitly embraces Shakespeare. Diane Long Hoeveler reads Walpole's foreword as an attack on the Enlightenment philosophy that set out to debunk supernaturalism in support of Shakespeare's 'native British genius' that allows the use of spectral devices.[77] It became widely recognised then that an English gothic strand of night scenes and ghosts could be found in Shakespeare's work. Ann Radcliffe and a host of Minerva Press writers would cite Shakespeare as chapter epigraphs and appropriate aspects of his plays. As Dale Townshend comments, 'What started in a Walpolean gesture of bardic protection,

---

74 Thomas Mathias, *The Pursuits of Literature*, vol. 4 (London: T. Becket, 1797), v.
75 Ibid., 87.
76 Peter Mortensen, *British Romanticism and Continental Influences: Writing in an Age of Europhobia* (Basingstoke: Palgrave Macmillan, 2004), 26–27.
77 Diane Long Hoeveler, *Gothic Riffs: Secularizing the Uncanny in the European Imaginary, 1780–1820* (Columbus: Ohio State University Press, 2010), 38.

veneration, and emulation ended up in the wholesale dispersal of the bard in the trash of the circulating libraries'.[78]

However, by following Gray's lead, Mathias believed he had identified a mine of national poetry that took its starting point in Norse verses and found a place in Shakespeare's writing. In the 1797 edition of *Pursuits of Literature*, Mathias consolidates the idea that the 'uncouth Runic phantasy' is a literary ancestor. This was a tradition whose images could be revitalised for the benefit of a faltering English literary practice that no longer hears the song of 'Death's sisters' (the Norns) or looks to 'Odin's magic tree', on which the god Odin sacrificed himself to learn the secret of the magic runes.[79] Mathias expresses a clear hope for the renewal of native poetics in the 1790 edition of *Runic Odes*: he wanted to 'transfuse the wild spirit of Norse poetry into the English language'.[80] For Mathias, Norse supernaturalism was more than just an antiquarian curiosity; it was a means to recuperate a vibrant vernacular tradition for Britain. Not everyone agreed, however. When Mathias first published his translations from Norse mythology in 1781, the *Monthly Review* deemed Norse verses too 'wild and monstrous' to be suitable for modern poetry, despite an occasional 'sublime and magnificent image'.[81] Amidst the lack of consensus regarding the incorporation of Norse poetry into modern English practice, it is undeniable that it presented the age with a distinctive form of artistic expression.

Conclusion

The argument presented in this chapter is that the interest in the Norse tradition was embraced to establish an authentic lineage for British poetry. This pursuit sought to assimilate Skaldic and Eddic poetry into English literary heritage. The cultural dispute in Britain between the 'sentimental' Ossian and the relatively unsentimental Norse poets intersected with the promotion of terror writing. In their superstitions, the Scandinavians encapsulated a myriad of frightful images. Yet it was precisely in these images that it was claimed that the salutary virtues of resolve and human vitality could be found, and, by embracing them, the shattered spirit of the modern world may be revived.

---

78 Dale Townshend, 'Gothic Shakespeare', in *A New Companion to the Gothic*, ed. David Punter (Hoboken, NJ: John Wiley & Sons, 2012), 38–63 (48). The Bard's role in the tradition has also been extensively examined in *Gothic Shakespeares*, ed. John Drakakis and Dale Townshend (Abingdon: Routledge, 2008).

79 Mathias, *Pursuits of Literature* (1797), 17.

80 Thomas James Mathias, 'Advertisement', in *Runic Odes from the Norse Tongue* (London: T. Becket, 1790).

81 Review of *Runic Odes* in *The Monthly Review* (December 1781): 426–27 (426).

It is pertinent here to examine verses by Thomas Gray, who, more than any other writer, popularised Norse tradition as a literary fashion in Britain. In Gray's philosophical poem 'The Alliance of Education and Government', which comprises a series of reflections on the proper development of humankind throughout history, we find a note to a line on the old Viking invaders. If usually seen as the scourge of Europe, Gray qualifies this perception in the following observation:

> Those invasions of effeminate Southern nations by the warlike Northern people, seem (in spite of all the terror, mischief, and ignorance which they brought with them) to be necessary evils; in order to revive the spirit of mankind, softened and broken by the arts of commerce, to restore them to their native liberty and equality, and to give them again the power of supporting danger and hardship; so a comet, with all the horrors that attend it as it passes through our system, brings a supply of warmth and light to the sun, and of moisture to the air.[82]

These verses address the ambiguous nature of the reception in British intellectual culture. If applied to literary tradition, it seems reasonable to suggest that Gray saw in the unyielding, unsentimental and sublimely horrible images of Norse poetry a remedy for modern softness and luxury. If the Old North was clearly horrific and terrible in many respects, when considered historically, it was also a catalyst for rekindling a weakened spirit to its native liberty and resilience. Transferred to the realm of literature, we find that an empowering sense of reviving salutary terrors existed. By embracing the horror of an ethno-national past, it was felt that new vitality was breathed into the cultural tapestry.

Just like one can identify a certain regularity in the representation of Orientalism, what became a recognisable 'Northernism' was the focus on dark, visceral and gory images. If 'terror' became a dominant paradigm in late eighteenth-century and early nineteenth-century reception of Norse mythology and poetry, it should be remembered that this was premised on the fact that only a sparse selection of material from the tradition was yet accessible in translation. It was only in the course of the nineteenth century that more nuances were firmly added to the general reception, such as through the publication of Esaias Tegnér's version of *Frithiof's Saga* (1825), which became a European success. Lecturing in 1840, Thomas Carlyle held Gray

---

82 *The Poems of Thomas Gray. To Which are Prefixed Memoirs of His Life and Writings by W. Mason*, vol. 1 (Dublin: D. Chamberlaine et. al., 1775), 197.

partly responsible for distorting the reception of Norse culture in Britain, not least by eclipsing its heroic imperatives with an unbalanced focus on elements of darkness. Thus, Gray purportedly prejudiced generations of readers to view Norse tradition as a 'gloomy palace of black ashlar marble, shrouded in awe and horror'.[83] Given the high level of interest in Gray's odes and the pioneering effort of the translations, this is not an entirely unfair assessment.

---

83 Thomas Carlyle, *On Heroes, Hero-worship, and the Heroic in History: Six Lectures* (London: Chapman and Hall, 1852), 55.

Chapter 2

BALLADS ACROSS BORDERS – TERRORS, TRANSLATIONS AND TRAVESTIES

This chapter will focus on the adaptations and imitations of Scandinavian ballads. These supernatural ballads helped make Scandinavia, particularly Denmark, a rich setting for the Gothic. Mapping this development is important, but the analysis addresses the underlying factors that led to the adaptation of Danish ballad material. The central author of the Gothicised ballad tradition was Matthew Lewis, who first incorporated a Danish ballad in *The Monk* and later selected several for his anthology *Tales of Wonder*. The chapter analyses how the ballad adaptations were bound up with Lewis' career and developments in the book market.

The Danish ballads were acknowledged as constituting a repository that was part of British cultural history. Hence, they could be exploited as Gothic texts facilitating a more immediate and profound connection with native literary heritage. While Norse culture represented a definitive past, allowing for the safe appreciation of its supernatural figures, folkloric practices derived from Scandinavia required more careful management. This was due to its association with superstitious irrationalism, which was perceived to be actively embraced and preserved within low culture. The chapter aims to provide insight into the treatment of folklore, offering an understanding of how the Danish material was approached and also satirised in the context of Gothic publishing.

From *The Monk* to *Tales of Wonder*

In Britain, the recovery of ballads gained momentum in the course of the eighteenth century. Editions of the Scottish collector Allan Ramsay's *Tea Table Miscellany* (first published in 1723) were popular, as was Thomas Percy's *The Reliques of Ancient English Poetry* (first published in 1765). Johann Gottfried Herder translated several English ballads from Percy's collection for his *Volkslieder* (1778–79). Herder's anthology also contains some important examples of Danish ballads, which will be discussed below. Herder translated six Norse songs (categorised as 'Skaldic') and five Danish ballads. Herder's objective with *Volkslieder* was to use songs from around Europe to represent the essential character of ethnic and national groups. The Danish ballads that Herder printed were taken from an anthology of 100 folk ballads, published by Danish historian Anders Sørensen Vedel in 1591, and updated in a new edition edited by the folklorist Peder Syv in 1695, doubling the number of ballads. There was a popular reprint of this work in 1739, to which Herder refers.[1]

In the first edition of Matthew Lewis' controversial *The Monk* (1796), he incorporated a version of one of the Danish ballads from Vedel/Syv's collection, which he had picked up from Herder's anthology ('Der Wasserman'). This was in the same year that several English translations of Gottfried August Bürger's imitation of a folk ballad, 'Lenore', created a sensation in Britain and helped establish ballads as middle-class entertainment after having previously being considered a 'low' form of folk culture. Where once they had served cultural functions and been spread orally, the ballads were now regarded primarily as objects of fascination for their lurid, macabre or superstitious content. Since literary Gothic interest in Danish balladry can be traced back to this adaptation, it is worth briefly outlining the framework in which it appears.

One of the minor characters in *The Monk* is Theodore, who pretends to be a beggar to enter the convent of St. Clare in Spain. Theodore uses this pretence because he suspects that Agnes, his master's sweetheart, has been incarcerated in its catacombs. Theodore endears himself to the nuns at the convent by telling outrageous stories about his travels around the world, such as his adventures among dog-headed men, and that he lost an eye by gazing upon a nude statue of the Virgin Mary. Throughout the novel, Lewis mocks what he sees as a Catholic tendency towards irrationalism. Theodore also embarks on a story about Denmark, to which one of the nuns asks: 'Are not the people all blacks in Denmark?' Theodore replies

---

1 *Et Hundrede Udvalde danske Viser* [...] *Forøgede med det andet hundrede Viser*, ed. Peder Syv (Copenhagen: J. P. Bockenhoffer, 1739). On the ballads, see Lis Møller, 'Travelling Ballads. The Dissemination of Danish Medieval Ballads in Germany and Britain, 1760s to 1830s, in *Danish Literature as World Literature*, eds. Dan Ringgaard and Mads Rosendahl Thomsen (London: Bloomsbury, 2017), 31–37; and Robert W. Rix, 'The European Circulation of Nordic Texts in the Romantic Period', *Oxford Research Encyclopedias: Literature* (2017), 8. https://doi.org/10.1093/acrefore/9780190201098.013.294.

that they are 'a delicate pea-green, with flame-coloured hair and whiskers'.[2] This claim riffs on the medieval geographical imagination about the North. For example, the eleventh-century German chronicler Adam of Bremen tells readers that, alongside dog-people with faces on their chests, there are pale-green people [*homines pallidi, virides*] living between the Gulf of Bothnia and furthest northeastern Europe.[3]

Theodore further tells the nuns that Denmark is 'terribly infested by sorcerers, witches, and evil spirits'.[4] The irony appears to be that the Catholic nuns are intrigued by this wayward superstition, which is essentially no less irrational than the beliefs attributed to the Catholic Church in the novel. Denmark is presented as a hub of demons that reign over the elements. There is an Erl- (or Oak-) King, a Fire-King, a Cloud-King and a Water-King each commanding a host of goblins, fairies or other imps. Theodore then sings a ballad about the Water-King because this is a song Agnes had taught him. He hopes she may give him a sign from within her prison by singing it. The ballad tells the story of a merman who dresses up as a knight to lure a maiden into marrying him. The maiden eventually drowns in the sea, as this is the merman's home. One interpretation drawn from this narrative is that aristocrats' promises can be deceitful and that there are dangers for vulnerable females whose trust is misplaced in the vows of those wielding social power through virtue of their rank alone.

Compared with the more faithful version of the ballad printed in Herder's *Volkslieder*, Lewis doubled the number of lines, expanding the two-line stanzas to four verses. In the process, the ballad is supercharged with elements of terror. Most prominently, he details the devious abduction of the maiden – her desperate plea for help when drowning is Lewis' invention. Furthermore, Lewis also makes the Water-King's seduction suggest sexual assault: '– "Stop! stop! for God's sake, stop! for oh! / "The waters o'er my bosom flow."' This element matches the subplot of another female character in *The Monk*: the young Antonia, who becomes infatuated with the seemingly noble Ambrosio, is drugged and raped in the crypt beneath his convent. In this way, Lewis manipulates the ballad to impart a meaningful connection to the themes of the novel.

---

2 Matthew Gregory Lewis, *The Monk: A Romance*, vol. 3 (London: J. Bell, 1796), 14.

3 See Rudolf Simek, 'Monstra septentrionalia: Supernatural Monsters of the Far North in Medieval Lore', in *Imagining the Supernatural North*, ed. Eleanor R. Barraclough, Danielle M. Cudmore and Stefan Donecker (Edmonton: University of Alberta Press, 2016), 55–75 (58).

4 Lewis, *The Monk*, 14.

If the success of Bürger's 'Lenore' sparked an interest in ballads more generally, Lewis' introduction of a Danish ballad established a parallel trajectory. The impact of Lewis' contribution is examined in this section. Lewis may have inspired the anonymous *Albert and Ellen. A Danish Ballad* (1797).[5] The poem, which has no relation to any Danish original, tells the story of a young woman abducted by a grim messenger of Odin. The emissary transports her to his master's hall so that she can marry the Norse god. However, Ellen boldly refuses Odin's proposal and pledges loyalty exclusively to her beloved Albert. The whole scenario turns out to be a dream; but, upon waking, Ellen discovers that Albert has died, leaving readers to speculate if his death may have been a consequence of her refusal. The references to Norse mythology are inspired by Thomas Percy's translation of Paul-Henri Mallet's work in *Northern Antiquities* (1770), which the author cites in a note. The literary ballad presents an interesting transitional form: the author resorts to Norse mythological material (not usually a characteristic of the ballad tradition) to make the imitation appear 'Danish'.

However, Lewis would himself expand the repertoire of Danish-themed ballads. The crowning glory of Gothicised ballads was his two-volume anthology, *Tales of Wonder*, published in 1800 (the imprint says 1801, but it was advertised for sale on 2 December 1800), published by the London bookseller Joseph Bell.[6] Volume I contains 32 poems by Lewis himself, Walter Scott, John Leyden and others. Volume II contains 28 poems reprinted from the works of older poets, such as Ben Johnson, Dryden, Burns, Glover and Harrington, as well as ballads from Percy's *Reliques of Ancient English Poetry*. Bell issued a second edition in one volume (imprint 1801), focusing on the more recent material, which reduced the number of poems to 32.

Several pieces specifically refer to Danish and Norse traditions. In Volume I, we find 'Elver's Hoh' (which Lewis marks as 'Danish'), 'The Sword of Angantyr' (marked as 'Runic'), 'King Hacho's Death-Song' (marked as 'Runic'), 'The Erl-King' ('founded on a Danish tradition'), 'The Erl-King's Daughter' (marked as 'Danish'), 'The Water-King' (marked as 'Danish') and 'The Cloud-King' (unmarked, but evidently an imitation of a Danish ballad). In Volume II, there are Thomas Gray's translations 'The Fatal Sisters' and 'The Descent of Odin' (both 'From the Norse tongue'). However, other ballads in Volume I also place Gothic narratives in the north of Europe. Lewis designates the ballad 'Sir Hengist'

5 *Edmund and Velina, a Legendary Tale. And Albert and Ellen, a Danish Ballad* (Edinburgh: Archibald Constable, 1797).

6 *Tales of Wonder*, ed. Matthew Lewis (London: J. Bell, 1801). Henceforth, this work will be referenced as *ToW* in brackets within the text.

as a translation from German in a short preamble, adding: '*I forget where I met the original of this Ballad*' (*ToW* 17). It is highly likely that this poem, like many others in the collection, was written by Lewis himself. According to the eighth-century historian Bede, Hengist was a warlord in the invasion of Britain in the fifth century. The ballad is about a meeting with a ghost near the river Weser (now northern Germany), that is before Hengist left for Britain. There are references to Odin and the Norse underworld of Hel (*ToW* 19). Robert Southey's ballad 'Donica' is set in Finland. The story revolves around the woman Donica, who, after her death, was possessed by the Devil for two years. Southey would return to a similar idea in *Thalaba the Destroyer* (1801), in which a demon takes over a lifeless girl's body and turns her into a type of vampire.

In Volume I, Norse- and Danish-themed ballads recuperate the Gothic from its usual focus on debauchery, which was roundly censured in the press. Furthermore, the Danish material was an authentic oral tradition closely linked to Britain. The endeavour to validate Gothic writing by placing it in historical frameworks is congruent with Franz J. Potter's observations of the need to justify Gothic publications as acceptable reading material.[7] Using authentic Norse and Danish examples was likely a deliberate strategy on Lewis' part to remove himself from the accusation of promoting immoral fantasies. It is interesting here to gauge the literary criticism of Nathan Drake, a staunch promoter of Norse-inspired poetry. In the 1798 edition of his *Literary Hours*, he includes the essay 'On Objects of Terror'. Here, he distinguishes between 'terror', which is an artful control of creating a thrilling sensation, and 'horror', which leads the reader to react with aversion and repulsion. The three examples Drake gives of 'horror' are a tale of a graverobber failing his crime after seeing the decayed corpse, a ballad about a son's execution of his father at the behest of his own mother; and Walpole's *The Mysterious Mother* (1768), which contains 'a mother's premeditated incest with her own son'.[8] Eric Parisot correctly identifies that what these examples have in common is that they are 'morally abhorrent'.[9] In another essay from *Literary Hours*, Drake praises Gray's Norse Odes (see Chapter 1), stating that the 'Gothic and

---

7 Franz J. Potter, *The History of Gothic Publishing, 1800–1835: Exhuming the Trade* (Houndsmills: Palgrave, 2005), 88. The period Potter discusses is slightly later (c. 1825–1834).

8 Nathan Drake, *Literary Hours: Or, Sketches Critical and Narrative* (London: T. Cadell and W. Davies, 1798), 246–47, (247).

9 Eric Parisot, 'The Aesthetics of Terror and Horror: A Genealogy', in *The Cambridge History of the Gothic*. Volume 1: *Gothic in the Long Eighteenth Century*, ed. Angela Wright and Dale Townshend (Cambridge: Cambridge University Press, 2020), 296.

Celtic superstitions [...] possess imagery peculiarly appropriate to the higher efforts of lyric composition'.[10] Taking Drake's literary distinction into account invites the plausible speculation that Lewis found in the Danish ballad material a subject matter that could shock and startle readers while not transgressing moral boundaries as had been the case in *The Monk*. If this was the purpose, it was partly successful. The *Anti-Jacobin Review* did see *Tales of Wonder* as an improvement and felt no urge to criticise this work. They commented that they thought Lewis was 'much better employed' in his new production than in *The Monk*, which had 'poison[ed] the fountains of morality' with its 'licentious' pursuits.[11]

However, in the review of *Tales of Wonder*, the *Critical Review* made a point of outright refusing to 'transcribe one couplet' (it was otherwise commonplace to provide samples of verse lines in reviews) because 'there is nothing but fiends and ghosts – all is hideous — all is disgusting'.[12] However, no indication of sexual immorality is indicated, so if Lewis' goal was to change direction in this regard, it was accomplished. The charge is rather against promoting supernaturalism, which is often inherent to the ballad form. This is explained in the following passage, which throws in a good dash of Europhobic nationalism:

> Instead of advancing in the glorious procession of truth and science, whose beams are daily gaining strength in our island, they [the contributors] turn with avidity to the errors of nations left far behind us in the gloom and darkness of barbarism, and are actually, in the nineteenth century, translating works from the northern languages, which, in the sixteenth, our better-informed ancestors would have been ashamed to have seen written in English.[13]

Reviving ballads as a literary form was a central objective of the Romantic period. Yet, it entailed an anachronistic projection of antiquated folk beliefs that had otherwise been purged from polite society. Romanticism was a movement that often sought out alternative values in the rural communities that modernity had passed by. In Carina Hart's terminology, the interest in ballads constitutes a 'negative nostalgia', because while there is a desire to recuperate a vanishing folk tradition, it was also clear that the tradition contained the retrogressive elements that threatened the aspirations

---

10 Drake, *Literary Hours*, 380.
11 Review of *Tales of Wonder*, in *The Anti-Jacobin Review* (March 1801): 322–23.
12 Review of *Tales of Wonder*, in *The Critical Review* (January 1802): 112.
13 Ibid., 111–12.

of modernity.[14] The contradictory dynamic of revival and abjection that forms 'negative nostalgia' is often implied in theoretical conceptions of the Gothic. The superstition exists as a hauntology, showing us a cultural spectre of that which cannot be entirely eradicated. During a period in British literature when writers attempted to recover traditional oral literature and rural culture (from the Ossian poems to Wordsworth's *Lyrical Ballads*), the Danish ballad emerged as a dark doppelgänger to this trend. When Lewis reactivated the superstitious ballads – updating, printing and circulating them – the danger was that their irrationalism could seep out and stain the present. In other words, promoting superstitious ballads threatened Britain's self-identification as a modern nation founded on Enlightenment and rationalism.

The fact that Northern superstitions could be found not only in the British past but also in the peripheries of contemporary Britain created the sense of a cultural palimpsest where the past continued to disrupt the sense of an ostensibly civilised and rational present. This is at the very heart of Gothic writing. Jerrold E. Hoggle, for example, describes the Gothic as a paradox which has 'come to connote a backward-leaning countermodernity [...] This retrogression appears to undermine [...] the assumption that the "modern" has left behind any regressive tendencies that might impede its progress'.[15] Jason Marc Harris, who has studied how folkish traditions were incorporated into English literature of the nineteenth century, writes that 'the rural network of folklore was a vibrant force that manifested a distinctive alternative voice to the emerging modernism of industrial progress and urbanization'.[16] In *Tales of Wonder*, we see a retrogressive movement back to the world of folk ballads for its capacity to disrupt prevailing modes of thought. However, it differs in mode and emphasis from Lewis' Romantic contemporary William Wordsworth. In his famous 'Preface' to *Lyrical Ballads* (1800), he wanted to emulate the language of the rural population, which he finds to be 'far more philosophical' than that produced in literary salons.[17] Wordsworth avows to temper the Gothic bent imported in the form of 'frantic novels' 'sickly and stupid German tragedies' and 'extravagant stories'.[18] The result was a collection of modern ballads suitable for a British readership. This left

---

14 Carina Hart, 'Gothic Folklore and Fairy Tale: Negative Nostalgia', *Gothic Studies* 22, no. 1 (2020): 1–13.

15 Jerrold E. Hoggle, 'Introduction: Modernity and the Proliferation of the Gothic', in *The Cambridge Companion to the Modern Gothic*, ed. Jerrold E. Hoggle (Cambridge: Cambridge University Press, 2014), 3–19 (4).

16 Jason Marc Harris, *Folklore and the Fantastic in Nineteenth-Century British Fiction* (London: Routledge, 2016), 15.

17 William Wordsworth, 'Preface', in *Lyrical Ballads, with Other Poems* (London: T. N. Longman and O. Rees, 1800), xii.

18 Ibid. xix.

S. T. Coleridge to provide what he describes in *Biographia Literaria* (1818) as 'directed to persons and characters supernatural', but the conservative and patriotic Coleridge now found himself 'averse to such subjects', as he reveals a year earlier in the preface to *Sibylline Leaves* (1817).[19]

Lewis savours the imports of Scandinavian terror, harnessing the superstitious beliefs to unearth aspects of the human condition that had been concealed or repressed by the structures of rational thought and social convention that defined his era. Whilst Wordsworth frequently engages with Gothic tropes and motifs within his ballads, he notably avoids using the full force of the Gothic aesthetic. Instead, he deflects and tempers the Gothic through various techniques, for example by often making them the effects of psychological misperception (as in 'The Thorn'). Lewis gives space to the supernatural, which could put him in the crosshairs of critics, as we see in the case of the *Critical Review*. The use of folklore from Denmark, a country seen by travellers and observers in the late eighteenth and early nineteenth to be on the periphery of Europe, and 'uncivilised' compared to Britain, only amplified the problem in the eyes of those who promoted modernity and rationalism as national values.[20]

Lewis' *Tales of Wonder* teeters between signalling antiquarian exploration of authentic tradition and exploiting material for its Gothic potential. Lewis may have seized on simultaneously pursuing two divergent options in relation to the presentation of 'The Water-King'. In the first editions of *The Monk*, 'The Water-King' is wholly absorbed into the fictional world of the novel, except for a short notice in the 'Advertisement' stating that the ballad 'from the third to the twelfth stanza' is 'the fragment of an original Danish ballad'.[21] However, in the fourth edition, retitled *Ambrosio, or The Monk. A Romance* (published in February 1798), Lewis changes tack. In a footnote, Lewis now informs the reader that not only the ballad is taken from Herder's collection of *Volkslieder*, but also that he, since publication, has met with two old Scottish ballads entitled 'May Colvin' (about a woman seduced by an elf-knight) and 'Clerk Colvill' (about a man seduced by a mermaid), which he claims bear 'a strong resemblance' to the Danish ballad.[22] (David Herd's anthology *Ancient and Modern Scottish Songs* from 1776 includes both ballads.)

---

19 For the citations, see Douglass H. Thomson, 'The Gothic Ballad', in *A New Companion to the Gothic*, ed. David Punter (Hoboken, NJ: John Wiley & Sons, 2012), 87.

20 On British perceptions of Scandinavian 'primitivism' from the late eighteenth century, see Dimitrios Kassis, *Representations of the North in Victorian Travel Literature* (Newcastle upon Tyne: Cambridge Scholars, 2015), esp. 12–20.

21 Advertisement in Matthew Lewis, *The Monk: A Romance* (London: J. Bell, 1796), vol. 1.

22 Matthew Lewis, *Ambrosio, or the Monk: A Romance*, vol. 3 (London: J. Bell, 1798), 18.

This paratext provides a context for the ballad that elevates it beyond what may initially seem like gratuitous terror, connecting it to a verifiable tradition of Germanic folklore. In this way, Lewis deliberately strikes a pose as a writer with an antiquarian interest. By drawing on references to Scottish tradition, he evokes a sense of *native* terror that touches closely on the reader's own cultural context, wielding folklore research as a new tool in his arsenal as a writer of terror.

The choice cannot be entirely separated from the accusations of plagiarism, which were levelled at Lewis soon after the publication of *The Monk*. The re-use of folk culture was a complicated matter, as Tilar J. Mazzeo has noted in connection with the critical attacks on Lewis for borrowing material (most critically in connection with the 'Bleeding Nun' tale). She argues that Lewis could not have been found guilty of 'culpable plagiarism', as this charge functioned in the Romantic period to prevent harm to an individual author's reputation. The folklore material Lewis exploited was 'authorless'; thus, it was rather a question of 'the degree to which Lewis had improved upon or assimilated his borrowed materials, which was another way of asking whether Lewis had succeeded or failed as an author'.[23] By rehabilitating the 'The Water-King' as an object of antiquarian interest, it became more than just an irreverent terror piece. Lewis' new-found framework for the ballad turned his borrowing into a more respectable Romantic-era pursuit of folklore, emphasising a commitment to recovering an ancestral tradition.

In Gothic writing, there is often an indeterminate play between what is original, an adaptation, and plagiarism. In reference to Lewis' 'Advertisement' in *The Monk*, where he lists some of his many influences/ borrowings from other works (including his use of the Danish ballad of 'The Water-King'), the *Monthly Review* was surprisingly positive:

> This may be called plagiarism, yet it deserves some praise. The great art of writing consists in selecting what is most stimulant from the works of our predecessors, and in uniting the gathered beauties into a new whole, more interesting than the tributary models.[24]

This returns us to Mazzeo's point about the adaptation of folklore material being less about culpable plagiarism and more about the ability of the adapter to turn old material into something eminently readable.

---

23 Tilar J. Mazzeo, *Plagiarism and Literary Property in the Romantic Period* (Philadelphia, PA: University of Philadelphia Press, 2007), 83.

24 Review of *The Monk*, in *The Monthly Review* (August 1797): 451.

In this respect, Lewis was keen to show that he was proficient in churning out effective terror writing. When 'The Water-King' was printed in *Tales of Wonder*, two years later, a note reads: 'As I have taken great liberties with this Ballad, and have been such questioned as to my share in it, I shall here subjoin a literal translation' (*ToW* 66). An alternative version is then provided, entitled 'The Water-Man', which is a translation that aligns more closely with Herder's German translation. Lewis presents a complex author persona by including an augmented version and a more literal rendition of the original ballad. He simultaneously embodies the role of the antiquarian, curating pieces from folklore tradition and that of the savvy and self-consciously brilliant author adept at crafting a spine-thriller. 'The Water-King' was successful beyond Lewis' own publications, as it was set to music by the English composer John Wall Calcott for a three-voice glee dated 26 January 1799, republished in Dublin by Hime and Gough in 1800 and by T. S. MacLean in 1820; and re-issued in London in 1856.[25]

Elves of Evil

Having explored Lewis' complex authorial presentation through his augmentation of 'The Water-King', I shall now examine how he adapted other Danish ballads. German poets J. W. Goethe and G. A. Bürger wrote *Kunstballaden*, i.e. imitations that often retained some of the same supernatural elements and diction as oral ballads, and there are a number of such ballads in *Tales of Wonder*. However, Lewis also elected to work from authentic source material (albeit through German translation). He does not remain strictly faithful to these pieces but engages in deft manipulations that transform them into reflections on recognisable Gothic tropes. In this way, Lewis subtly positions the ballad form as ripe for reconceptualisation through a Gothic lens. It is to such subtle adaptations that I now turn.

The first Danish ballad in *Tales of Wonder* (in order of appearance) is 'Elver's Hoh', which first appeared in print in the Vedel/Syv collection. It is usually categorised as a 'magical ballad' (*Tryllevise*) of which only 82 unique examples are extant in the Danish tradition. The magical ballads contain supernatural beings and incidents. In Lewis' version of the poem, a weary knight falls asleep on a hill and is awakened by elf-maidens who attempt to lure him into joining their dance and teach him their magic. The knight, realising their

---

25 See Roger Hansford, *Figures of the Imagination: Fiction and Song in Britain, 1790–1850* (London: Routledge, 2017), 119.

sinister intentions, is relieved when he hears a cock crow, and they disappear. Lewis is careful to describe the provenance of the ballad in a headnote:

> The original is to be found in the 'Kiampe-Viiser,' Copenhagen, 1739. My version of this Ballad (as also of most of the Danish Ballads in this collection) was made from a German translation to be found in Herder's 'Volkslieder'. (*ToW* 31)

However, Lewis fails to mention that there is a gap in the transmission from original to English translation insofar as Herder writes in a note to the ballad that 'the magic of the original is untranslateable'.[26] On this account, Lewis perhaps felt encouraged to produce an imaginative verisimilitude of the poem rather than attempt a faithful translation. Generally, the disconnection from authentic ancient magic beliefs seems to drive Lewis to reimagine and reconstruct Danish folklore magic in his ballads, as we shall see below. This creative reconfiguration of a lost magical system allows him to craft evocative supernatural narratives that speak to the anxieties of his own time while drawing on the perceived power of bygone nature mystery. In the ballads, Lewis found a new iteration of the theme he had pursued in *The Monk*: the fascination with how individuals may succumb to temptations, including sexual desire, pride, and the allure of the supernatural.

Another Lewis adaptation of a Danish ballad is 'The Erl-King's Daughter', also sourced from Herder's *Volkslieder*, where it has the title *Erlkönigs Tochter*. The narrative concerns Sir Oluf, who is tempted by the Elf-King's daughter. Despite her offer of gold, he refuses to join her because he is to be married the next day. Sir Oluf takes leave but is cursed by the spiteful elf. He later dies from sickness, leaving bereft his wife-to-be. If one consults Jacob Grimm's monumental nineteenth-century work on Germanic mythology, elves had the ability to make people and animals sick or even cause death through their touch or breath.[27] The ballad is an illustration of this. However, from the perspective of an early nineteenth-century culture already steeped in decades of Gothic romance publications, 'The Erl-King's Daughter' can be interpreted according to a recognisable motif of suffering and potential death linked to unrequited desire. If the body became increasingly 'readable' with the development of medical science, the notion that psychological forces could foster illness gained importance. Illness is seen as an effect of repressed desire in William Blake's 'The Sick Rose' (1794), and John Keats explores

---

26 Johann Gottfried von Herder, *Volkslieder*, vol. 1 (Leipzig: Weygand, 1778), 322.
27 Jacob Grimm, *Teutonic Mythology*, trans. James Steven Stallybrass, vol. 2 (London: George Bell and Sons, 1883), 460.

how a cold woman creates misery in his fake medieval ballad, 'La Belle Dame sans Merci' (1819). Lewis was willing to project illicit desire and temptation as symbolic supernatural characters, as we also see in connection with the Devil and his emissaries in *The Monk*. If Ambrosio is piqued by supernatural characters, we should not forget that it is also a battle that takes place in his inner 'theatre of a thousand contending passions'.[28]

It is possible that Lewis was drawn to the Scandinavian elves as representations of the destructive power of desire. They replace the Christian references to satanic influences with those of these mythical folklore creatures, who also lead men to ruin through their desires. One may here be reminded of a note to the translation of the Edda, in which Paul-Henri Mallet explains that the 'evil Fairies' mentioned in the mythology are the 'bud and germ' of ancient folklore superstitions, as 'Gothic tribes' had a great veneration for 'Fairies or Destinies' who were believed to hold 'every man's fate was in their hands'.[29] Diane Long Hoeveler's analysis of the ballad form is pertinent here. She describes it as a venue where 'a debate is played out between the residual claims of the primitive, blood culture, and the new enlightened forces of rationality of the individualized and modern subject'.[30] The revival of the ballad is, therefore, a core Gothic pursuit. For Lewis, as for other British adapters of ballads, there is a compelling psychological allure to mining Scandinavian tradition for insights into their own ethno-Gothic cultural past. It allows them to confront repressed facets of human nature that modernity and rationalism had eradicated from mainstream thought. The supernatural elements found in Danish folklore can be seen as proxies for the primitive facets of the self. By engaging with Danish legend, it is possible to rediscover parts of the psyche in an externalised manner. In this context, Danish balladry serves as both a cultural and introspective lens. The question is why Danish balladry, in particular, held representational significance within British cultural frameworks at the time.

Several of the poems in *Tales of Wonder* are 'translations'. Addressing this aspect, Jayne Winter writes of Lewis that he 'used the concept of translation to exploit his readers' expectation of the sensational and fear of the foreign'.[31]

---

28 Lewis, *Ambrosio, or The Monk* (1798), 141.
29 Paul-Henri Mallet, *Northern Antiquities: Or, a Description of the Manners, Customs, Religion and Laws of the Ancient Danes, and Other Northern Nations; Including Those of Our Own Saxon Ancestors*, trans. Thomas Percy, 2 vols (London: T. Carnan and Co., 1770), 2:54.
30 Diane Long Hoeveler, *Gothic Riffs: Secularizing the Uncanny in the European Imaginary, 1780–1820* (Columbus, OH: Ohio State University Press, 2010), 181.
31 Jayne Winter 'International Traditions: Ballad Translations by Johann Gottfried Herder and Matthew Lewis', *German Life and Letters* 67, no. 1 (2014): 22–37 (35).

The Danish settings in the ballads were a way to posit a culture where people would believe that evil supernatural beings ruled their lives. However, I will contend that Lewis does not consider the Danish ballads as just foreign specimens. Diane Long Hoeveler has proposed that the collection was born out of a desire to 'forge nothing less than an alternative supernatural literary genealogy for British poetry, one that seamlessly incorporated the Germanic as part of its heritage, rather than as a "foreign importation"'.[32] Thus, it may be more accurate to understand Lewis as leveraging them for their intriguing capacity for *Verfremdung*. Through the slightly defamiliarising lens of Danish folk tradition, Lewis was able to cast a fresh light on supernatural motifs and storytelling that were already known from Percy's *Reliques of Ancient English Poetry*. However, the connection of these ballads to Britain would have been clear to most readers.

To understand Lewis' interest in Danish balladry, it is essential to note the connection that allegedly existed between Anglo-Saxon culture and its Scandinavian roots. The links were often most clearly articulated in relation to Scotland. Thus, the Danish ballads, despite being translated from another language, came to be regarded as an integral part of British cultural heritage. Rather than being seen as an exotic import, they provide a window into the past, offering a glimpse of the beliefs and traditions suppressed by the urbanised modern state. For example, in his two-volume *Popular Ballads and Songs from Tradition [...] With Translations of Similar Pieces from the Ancient Danish Language* (1806), the Scottish antiquarian Robert Jamieson printed versions of the same Danish ballads that Lewis had translated, stating that he has 'no ambition to rival Mr. Lewis'.[33] In contrast to the Gothicisation of the ballads, Jamieson worked directly from Danish sources and aimed at a Scottish 'nationalisation' of them. The titles he gives the ballads are 'The Mer-Man', 'Elfer Hill' and 'Sir Oluf and the Elf King's Daughter'. The ballads are cast in a distinctly Scottish idiom, what Jamieson refers to as 'Albinizing Scandinavian poetry'.[34] Jamieson reconstructs what a Scottish version of the Danish ballads would have sounded like if it had been recorded in Scotland and not in Denmark. For example, Jamieson has the maiden in 'The Mer-Man' look desirously at her soon-to-be seducer with the wish: 'God gif that gude knicht were

---

32 Diane Long Hoeveler, *Gothic Riffs: Secularizing the Uncanny in the European Imaginary, 1780–1820* (Columbus: Ohio State University Press, 2010), 165.

33 Robert Jamieson, *Popular Ballads and Songs: From Tradition, Manuscripts and Scarce Editions; with Translations of Similar Pieces from the Ancient Danish Language, and a Few Originals by the Editor*, vol. 1 (Edinburgh: A. Constable and Company, 1806), 208.

34 Ibid., 208–209.

for me'; while the merman calls out to his future wife to 'gang wi' me!'[35]
Jamieson was a close friend of Walter Scott, who would praise him for
his discovery of the kinship between Danish and Scottish ballad tradition,
referring to it as 'a circumstance which no antiquary had hitherto so much
as suspected'.[36]

In *Minstrelsy of the Scottish Border* (first published in 1802), Scott himself
collected ballads mixed in with new imitations. In an essay connected with
his retelling of the old Scottish ballad tale of Tamlane, he explores the rich
tradition of fairy belief, emphasising that the English elf finds its prototype
in the Scandinavian *berg-elfen* (mountain elves).[37] Scott also incorporated an
adaptation of a Danish ballad (which Jamieson had shown him in a literal
translation) in his long narrative poem *The Lady of the Lake* (1810). The ballad
concerns a man who is turned into a monster by the Elfin King, but the man
is freed from this curse when he is blessed three times. In a long note, Scott
explains that the story is similar to the border ballad of 'The Young Tamlane'
but that several other examples from the English-Scottish border find 'exact
counterparts' in the Danish ballads'.[38]

The link between Scandinavian and British traditions was discussed
in several places during the period, and it was a primary reason for adapting
Danish balladry, as we see it, for example, in connection with the English poet
Rose Lawrence's 'Elric and Elsee: A Danish Ballad' (1829), which was based
on genuine source material (albeit second-hand).[39] The story concerns Elsee,
whose sorrow over Elric's death calls him back from the dead. The spectral
return of the lover does not end well, however, as he leads her to join him
in the grave. The ballad adaptation appeared alongside sentimental poetry
taken from various traditions worldwide. This is a testament to female
participation in cosmopolitan culture, yet the Danish ballad also speaks
to a British context. Lawrence notes that the superstitious admonishment
against excessive mourning was 'probably common' to 'northern nations',

---

35 Ibid., 211.

36 Walter Scott, 'Introductory Remarks on Popular Poetry', in *The Lay of the Last Minstrel,
    and Marmion* (Edinburgh: Adam and Charles Black, 1869), 537–51 (550).

37 Walter Scott, 'Introduction to the Tale of Tamlane. On the Fairies of Popular
    Superstition', in *Minstrelsy of the Scottish Border*, vol. 2 (Edinburgh: James Ballantyne,
    1810), 109–86 (110).

38 Walter Scott, *The Lady of the Lake: A Poem* (Edinburgh: John Ballantyne, 1810), 366.

39 Rose Lawrence, *The Last Autumn at a Favourite Residence: With Other Poems* (London:
    G. and J. Robinson; and Longman, Rees, Orme, Brown & Green, 1829), 38–44.
    Lawrence borrowed the ballad from the 1810 play *Axel and Valborg* by the Danish poet
    and playwright Adam Oehlenschläger, probably through its German translation.

and this can be seen from the empirical evidence collected in Anne Grant's two-volume early ethnographic book *Essays on the Superstitions of the Highlanders of Scotland* (1811).[40]

The notion of an affiliation linking the folkloric traditions of Denmark and Britain was propagated in scholarly circles throughout the nineteenth century. An evaluation of the numerous compelling arguments for a substantial Scandinavian influence on Britain was provided by R. C. Alexander Prior, an English author, translator and antiquarian. In the introduction to his translation of *Ancient Danish Ballads* (1860), he refers to the Anglo-Saxons as constituting 'one nation' with the Danes 'before the immigration of our ancestors to this island'.[41] This statement refers back to the idea of a common ethno-Gothic foundation of the Scandinavians and the Anglo-Saxon invaders-cum-settlers of Britain. Prior notes that while most of Europe had abandoned traditional ballads, they were preserved in Scandinavia and Scotland 'as great favourites with the people, as ever they were'.[42] In the early decades of the nineteenth century, there was an ongoing effort to ground supernatural narratives in traditional folklore, highlighting how the Gothic was more than just modern sensationalism.

In this respect, the Danish tradition was frequently referred to as a foundational layer of superstition disseminated across northern nations. In the collection *Legends of Terror!: And Tales of the Wonderful and Wild* (1826; new ed. 1830), a prose account entitled 'The Chase of King Waldemar, The Dane', which is 'taken from the popular traditions and superstitions of Danes', tells the story of a king who was punished by higher forces to become a restless phantom rider in the woods.[43] The headnote to this text proposes the theory that the legend may be 'the true foundation' of G. A. Bürger's famous ghost ballad 'Der Wilde Jäger', and that many 'romantic legends which are now or have been highly popular in Germany' may trace their origin to 'the superstitious relics and oral traditions of Danes, Norwegians, and other northern nations'.[44] A translation of Bürger's ballad entitled 'The Chase' and a version of his 'Leonore' with the anglicised title 'William and Helen' became Walter Scott's debut publication in 1796.

---

40 Ibid., 38.
41 Richard Chandler Alexander Prior, 'Introduction', in *Ancient Danish Ballads*, vol. 1 (London: Williams and Norgate, 1860), xiii.
42 Ibid., xi.
43 *Legends of Terror!: And Tales of the Wonderful and Wild* (London: Sherwood, Gilbert, and Piper, 1826), 348.
44 *Legends of Terror* also contains 'The Mountain King. A Swedish Legend' (p. 349), based on a folk story from Scandinavia about a young woman who weds a king who resides in a supernatural realm within a mountain.

The Elemental Kings of Denmark

In the previous chapter, it was noted that Samuel Johnson claimed Shakespeare had incorporated 'the Gothick mythology of fairies' into *A Midsummer Night's Dream*. In utilising the mythology of the Danish ballad tradition, Lewis may well have looked to this play. Shakespeare describes Oberon as the 'king of fairies' who rules over other spirits of nature and as a figure of mischief and mayhem for humans. In Lewis' ballad sequel to Shakespeare's play, 'Oberon's Henchman, or The Legend of the Three Sisters' (1808), he refers to 'all the sprights of earth, air, fire, and sea!'[45] This is the system of fairy lore that Lewis imposes (with no basis in the source material) on Danish folklore in *The Monk* (conveyed through Theodore's description of Denmark). The young Walter Scott was the first to pick up on Lewis' cue in his 1799 collection *An Apology for Tales of Terror*, which was given a limited print run (only 12 copies were printed). Scott's reason for publishing was his frustration with Lewis' tardiness in completing the promised *Tales of Wonder*.[46] Scott included his own version of 'The Erl-King' alongside Lewis' translations of 'The Erl-King's Daughter' and 'The Water-King'. In relation to these, Scott refers to 'certain mischievous Spirits' who 'preside over the different Elements' and inflict 'calamities on Man' to amuse themselves.[47] These are the 'ERL or OAK-KING', the 'WATER-KING', the 'FIRE-KING', and the 'CLOUD-KING'.[48] These represent the classical four elements (with wood standing in for earth) and seem to borrow from Paracelsus, who presented a comprehensive system of *homines spirituales* – beings associated with the four elements. This system was also made famous through Abbé de Montfaucon de Villars' strange 1670 work *Le Comte de Gabalis*. The conception Lewis promotes in his works of demonic fairies suggests an attempt to articulate a universe seemingly under the covert dominion of all-encompassing supernatural forces capable of deciding the fates of humans according to sinister, inscrutable designs.

In *Tales of Wonder*, Lewis manipulates the Danish ballads, which he had only seen in limited selections through Herder's translations, into a scheme that reveals a veritable demonology of malignant spirits. This is how a sense of coherence is established throughout the diverse poems. Lewis already had

---

45 Matthew Lewis, *Romantic Tales*, vol. 3 (London: Longman, Hurst, Rees, and Orme, 1808), 262.
46 D. L. Macdonald, *Monk Lewis: A Critical Biography* (Toronto: University of Toronto Press, 2000), 151.
47 Walter Scott, ed., *Apology for Tales of Terror* (Kelso: Printed at the Mail Office, 1799), 1.
48 Ibid., 1.

poems about the Water-King (not referred to as a 'king' in the sources) and the Erl-King. So, to fulfil the scheme of four elemental spirits, Lewis had to come up with ballads about fire and air. He asked Scott to compose the poem 'The Fire-King', a medievalist ballad that tells the story of Count Albert, a Christian knight who obtains a magic sword and participates in a crusade in the Holy Land. In a letter to Scott from 3 February 1800, Lewis writes that he objects to this figure 'being removed from his native land, Denmark, to Palestine'.[49] The poet John Leyden answered the call to contribute to the collection with a poem about a Cloud-King, but Lewis did not think his image of the evil spirit was majestic enough.[50] Thus, it was included in the collection under the new title 'The Elfin-King'. It is interesting that Leyden's references to the 'Green Knight', moors, the 'morrice' dance and the 'Northern lights' (*ToW* 182–93) point to a Scottish setting, thus once again underscoring the connection between Scandinavia and Scotland. As we will see below, Lewis himself provided a ballad of a Cloud-King. Generally, there is a focus on landscapes in the ballads. The place of the Gothic scene has shifted from the dark castle's subterranean passageways to the forest or other areas where humanity does not exert control. Lewis creates a dark alternative to the idealistic appraisal of country beliefs that Wordsworth promotes as growing out of 'the beautiful and permanent forms of nature', as he writes in the celebrated 'Preface' to *Lyrical Ballads* (1800).[51] Lewis makes Denmark a *locus terribilis*. This was something we also see in Germany, where Benedikte Naubert, a writer of fairy tales, wrote a tale based in Denmark, on the island of Zealand, entitled *Erlkönigs Tochter*. It is mentioned here because it was translated as 'The Erl-King's Daughter' and included in *Popular Tales and Romances of the Northern Nations*, an anthology of German stories in three volumes, published in 1823.[52] Naubert invents a fictive island called Erl-Island, which is part of the Danish kingdom. The protagonist, Holm, almost perished due to falling prey to the strange spells of that place. Apart from the Erl-King and his daughter (called Edda), there is no reference to the ballad material. It shows us, however, that the knowledge of the Danish ballads had established Denmark as a scene of folkloric magic and dangerous seduction.

---

49 'Extracts from the Correspondence of M. G. Lewis', in Walter Scott, *The Poetical Works*, vol. 4 (Edinburgh: Ballantyne, 1838), 79–87 (85).
50 Ibid.
51 Wordsworth, 'Preface', xi.
52 [Benedikte Naubert], 'The Erl-King's Daughter', in *Popular Tales and Romances of the Northern Nations*, vol. 3 (London: W. Simpkin et al., 1823), 251–349. The name of the translator is not known.

Lewis wanted the supernatural to be front and centre in *Tales of Wonder*. For example, he wrote a letter to Walter Scott in 1798, explaining his plan for the collection: a 'ghost or a witch is a sine-qua-non ingredient in all the dishes of which I mean to compose my hobgoblin repast'.[53] The playfulness with which Lewis describes his intention carries over into *Tales of Wonder*. In fact, the mingling of serious and comic Gothic elements is evident throughout *Tales of Wonder*. Douglass H. Thomson sees the ballads as exploiting the genre's instability to satisfy the appetite for terror while also playfully spurning this appetite.[54] Additionally, the humour may aim to alleviate alarmist concerns about the Gothic's debauched and potentially antisocial themes, implying that critics of the genre are overreacting to something not meant to be taken seriously.

An example of satire is 'The Cloud-King,' an imitation of a Danish ballad, which has no source text. It is the fourth and last of the 'Danish' elemental kings in the order of appearance in volume 1 of *Tales of Wonder*. Thus, it may function as the satyr plays presented directly after the tragic trilogy in ancient Greece. These satyr plays were the reversal of Attic tragedy, a sort of 'jocular tragedy'. 'The Cloud-King' tells the story of an elemental fiend who rules the air over Denmark and Norway (united under the same crown then). The Cloud-King lusts after Lady Romilda, who lives in a 'Rosenhall' castle – perhaps a reference to Rosenholm Castle in Jutland, a peninsula Lewis mentions in the ballad. Alternatively, Lewis may be thinking of Rosenborg Castle in Copenhagen, specifically mentioned in a Danish grammar book for Englishmen, published in 1799.[55] Whether Lewis acquired this grammar book is far from certain, but grammar is a central issue in the ballad. The Cloud-King abducts Romilda with the intention of marrying her. At a pre-wedding celebration, with visitors, including the Water-King and the Erl-King, Romilda is served 'the head of a child' (*ToW* 83), one of the elements emphasising the hyperbolic terror. Before the marital union can take place, the Cloud-King must agree to obey two of Romilda's commands. The first is to show her the *'truest'* of her lovers, which the Cloud-King acts upon by magically summoning Romilda's doting page, Amorayn. Romilda's canny second command is to show her a *'truer'* love. The grammatical impossibility of placing a comparative after

53 Cited by Brett Rutherford, 'Introduction to Volume II', in Matthew Lewis, *Tales of Wonder*, vol. 2, 2nd ed. (Pittsburgh, PA: Poet's Press, 2017), xii–xvi (xii).
54 Douglass H. Thomson, 'Mingled Measures: Gothic Parody in *Tales of Wonder* and *Tales of Terror*', *Romanticism and Victorianism on the Net* no. 50 (2008), <https://id.erudit.org/iderudit/018143ar>.
55 Christian Frederik Schneider, *Danish Grammar Adapted to the Use of Englishmen* (Copenhagen: F. Brummer, 1799), 153.

a superlative leaves the Cloud-King unable to offer himself to Romilda. Defeated, he angrily returns Romilda to her castle to marry Amorayn.

In a concluding note, Lewis explains that the lady 'would infallibly have been devoured by the daemon, had she not luckily understood the difference between the comparative and superlative degrees' (*ToW* 87). Thus, female education here disrupts the Cloud-King's evil design. Judith Wilt has pointed out that a 'pure Gothic' convention is the 'exercise of power by the knowing over the ignorant', a trait in novels featuring women held captive by aristocratic tyrants. In Lewis' first unfinished novel, 'The Effusions of Sensibility', the heroine Honoria makes an ironic remark on female learning: 'The display of a woman's knowledge is, I know, generally esteemed ostentatious and disagreeable'.[56] Thus, Lewis already understood the subversive potential of female education. In a more general sense, he highlights the triumph of good middle-class education over traditional beliefs, sending a message to the readers – and surely also to his expected critics – that rational thinking will overcome superstition.

New Tales of Terror

To capitalise on the attention Lewis' *Tales of Wonder* received, his publisher Joseph Bell brought out the anonymous collection *Tales of Terror*, published in May 1801. It was long thought that Lewis was also the editor of these ballads, but no external evidence supports this claim.[57] This collection is interesting because it picks up on the Scandinavian references. Already in the 'Introductory Dialogue', it is evident that this Scandinavian terror was a marketable theme: 'The enraptured mind with fancy loves to toil / O'er rugged Scandinavia's martial soil'.[58] The introduction also mentions 'Lapland's snows' and that the mind may find guilty delight in imagining 'the blood-stained feasts of Odin's hall' as well as Danish pirates who plough the sea.[59]

The Norse references are expanded in the second ballad of the collection, 'Hrim Thor or The Winter King. A Lapland Ballad'. The name 'Hrim Thor' recalls the Norse *Hrimthursar* (Frost Giants) in the Poetic Edda, and the ballad

---

56 Judith Wilt, *Ghost of the Gothic* (Princeton: Princeton University Press, 1980), 138; Kerstin-Anja Münderlein discusses this passage in *Genre and Reception in the Gothic Parody: Framing the Subversive Heroine* (New York: Routledge, 2021), 145.

57 For identification of the collection with the architectural historian George Downing Whittington, see Mark Nicholls, '*Tales of Terror*, 1801', *Notes and Queries* NS 48, no. 2 (2001): 119–21.

58 *Tales of Terror* (Dublin: John Brooke, 1801), 6.

59 Ibid.

adds another elemental 'king' to the *faux* folklore mythology established in *Tales of Terror*. The poem tells the story of a young woman named Tura, who is lured away by a winter demon disguised as a courteous knight. They journey on horseback into a wintry wilderness. Tura finally realises she has been deceived but too late. Her cries are drowned in '[t]hick snows [...] and tempests howl' while 'loud exults the Winter-Sprit'.[60] The ballad's setting in Lapland is not coincidental, as this was a place associated with black magic and witchcraft. One may only think of Shakespeare's 'Lapland sorcerers' or John Milton's 'Lapland witches'. The painter Henry Fuseli alluded to the latter's lines in the title of his oil painting *The Night-Hag Visiting the Lapland Witches* (c. 1796), and William Wordsworth and John Keats also mentioned Lapland when wanting to evoke a sense of terror.[61] In Anne Bannerman's 1802 collection *Tales of Superstition and Chivalry*, the poem 'The Fisherman of Lapland' tells the tale of Peter who one night sees a shadowy figure in the snow, only to drown in the frosty billows later.[62]

Tales of Terror contains a selection of ballads cast as Spanish, Scottish, Welsh, Provençal, etc. Others have a Scandinavian setting such as 'The Sprite of the Glen: A Swedish Romance'. This is a supernatural tale about the young maiden, Bertha, from the castle Karlofelt near the mountains of Sevo.[63] A knight arrives at her window, declaring himself to be her lover, Geraldus. In this respect, the poem imitates the *topos* categorised in the Aarne-Thompson motif index as type 365: the Spectre Bridegroom. The verse lines describe the flight through a gloomy landscape. When the couple stop to declare their love for each other, the real Geraldus overhears them and strikes Bertha with a deadly blow for her seeming betrayal. The knight reveals himself to be the hideous Sprite of the Glen: 'his form so gigantic all reeking with gore, / A rough shaggy mantle of bear skin he wore, / Malignity scowl'd in his features so ghast, / His broad sable pinions he waved in the blast'.[64] Sweden was not a commonly used location for the Gothic. However, in 1801 Minerva Press brought out Anna Marie Mackenzie's *Swedish Mysteries, or, Hero*

---

60 *Tales of Terror*, 20.
61 For the image of Lapland, see Linda Andersson Burnett, 'Selling the Sami: Nordic Stereotypes and Participatory Media in Georgian Britain', in *Communicating the North: Media Structures and Images in the Making of the Northern Region*, ed. Jonas Harvard and Peter Stadius (Farnham: Ashgate, 2013), 171–96.
62 [Anne Bannerman], *Tales of Superstition and Chivalry* (London: Vernor and Hood, 1802), 91–96.
63 *Saevo* is the name of a mountain range mentioned in connection with the island of *Scatinavia* by the first-century Roman geographer Pliny the Elder in his *Naturalis Historia* (4.13.96).
64 *Tales of Terror*, 128.

of the Mines. The novel is full of dark mysteries but belongs in the category of 'explained supernatural'.[65]

A ballad that returns the scene to Denmark is 'The Wolf-King or Little Red-Riding-Hood. An Old Woman's Tale', which is a versified version of Charles Perrault's 1697 version of 'Little Red Riding Hood'. However, it is a travesty of the debauched taste with which Danish ballads had become associated: the wolf 'oped his jaws all sprent with blood / And fell on small Red riding hood / He tore out bowels one and two / – "Little maid I will eat you!" –'.[66] In *Tales of Terror*, the burlesque imitation (which is the hallmark technique of literary travesty) targets the grim demises often faced in the Danish ballads. This is seen in the accompanying illustration of the wolf gutting the grandmother of her intestines by the caricaturist Henry William Bunbury. This brings the story into line with the explicit violence of tearing and mangling that Lewis describes the Erl-King practising. The ballad furthermore re-invents the wolf as a 'king' to appropriate the tale into the scheme of evil rulers from *Tales of Wonder*. A short epigraph states that the ballad is a homage to Lewis (which it clearly is, albeit as a grotesque travesty of his style) but also adds that it was 'translated from the Danish' (which it most surely was not).[67] What is most interesting about this poem, however, is the author's attempt to provide a satirical perspective – not only on Lewis' invention of the elemental 'kings' who would terrorise Denmark but also on the critics who saw Lewis and his ilk as a danger to public order. In a note to the ballad, the author writes:

> Though the northern states of Europe are not conceived, even by the most violent alarmists, to be much infected by the principles of Jacobinism, yet in their *disloyal* languages '*King*' is often used as a term for a *fiend*, whose business is to destroy the happiness of mankind, and whose delight is in human misery.

The satire addresses the widely accepted idea, promoted by Paul-Henri Mallet, that the people of the North were unusually wedded to the ideal of freedom, disallowing any kind of tyranny. One reason for this was that the cold was a 'climate made for liberty', which made the people of Scandinavia triumph

---

65 See Janina Nordius, ed., 'Introduction' in *Swedish Mysteries, or, Hero of the Mines* (Kansas City: Valancourt Books 2008), vii–xxx. In 1815, another Gothic novel with a Swedish setting was published under the title: *The Curse of Ulrica; or The White Cross Knights of Riddarholmen. A Swedish Romance of the Sixteenth Century* (London: Black, Parry, and Company).

66 *Tales of Terror*, 27.

67 Ibid., 22.

over 'despotic sway'.[68] Scandinavia's purportedly incarnate love of liberty is utilised to mock the alarmist tendency among detractors of foreign imports. In 1799, for example, the *Anti-Jacobin*, a magazine aimed at countering radicalism, published *The Rovers*, a political satire with a serious message. In response to the English translation of Schiller's *The Robbers*, the German school of writing is accused of telling stories of 'how prime Ministers are shocking things, / And *reigning Dukes* as bad as tyrant Kings'.[69] The author of 'The Wolf-King' answers this type of attack with a dose of counter-satire, parodying conservative fears that foreign Gothic tales posed a threat to British society.

When even a folktale such as Little Red Riding Hood, ensconced in oral traditions around Europe, is turned into satire, it is clear that the limits of both ballad imitations and the Gothic mode have been reached. This is reflected upon in the *Poetical Register*, which generally praises *Tales of Wonder*. However, the reviewer is confused about how to read the ballads, noting that 'many of the tales are evidently designed to ridicule the present taste for the wonderful and of others, it is difficult to decide whether they are meant to be serious or ludicrous'.[70] Evidently, the balance Lewis had managed between folklore supernaturalism and its dismantling in satire is tipped in *Tales of Terror*, robbing the material of its impact by blunting the subversiveness of folk beliefs as a threat to social and religious order and replacing it with literary travesty.

Conclusion

The revival of the 'Danish' ballad in English translation must be understood against the backdrop of the Romantic period's general revival of the ballad form as a way of seeking authentic cultural expressions by looking back to folk beliefs. However, as Lewis discovered when writing *The Monk*, in which 'The Water-King' first appeared, ballads that once informed communities could be remade as sensationalised Gothic pieces to be savoured by middle-class readers. In this manner, the traditional ballads found new audiences, and their core purpose for traditional societies was transformed through a Gothicising lens. Unlike in *The Monk*, the folklore ballads provided Lewis with a new literary avenue that may still have focused on sexual desire but did not cross any taboo boundaries. When *Tales of Wonder* was published, the Danish material

---

68 Mallet, *Northern Antiquities*, 1:168.
69 'The Rovers', *The Beauties of the Anti-Jacobin: or, Weekly Examiner* (London: C. Chapple, 1799), 251–79 (252).
70 Review of *Tales of Wonder*, in *Poetical Register* 1 (1801): 437.

was sufficiently obscure to British readers, and Lewis himself had only access to a few specimens in German translation. Thus, seizing upon the material offered an imaginative opportunity to create a system of elemental evil that preys on humans to destroy them and pass it off as genuine folklore. Lewis manipulates and expands Danish balladry to fashion a terrifying meta-story that amplifies the terror element. The fabrication of this system of elemental fiends served to conjure the notion of an older supernatural universe that governed human fate and fortune. Essentially, it is a reconfiguration of the temptation orchestrated by the Devil in Lewis' *The Monk*, but the tale of human weakness is here transposed to folkloric legends, seen as deriving from the recesses of ethno-Gothic tradition. By interweaving ancient ethnic myths with tales of individuals ruined by lust or greed, Lewis places dual emphasis on exploring deeply buried aspects of human psychology. These were depths concealed by the veneer of civilised and polite society. Exploring the repressed underpins the literary Gothic, and we may understand the ballads as part of this context.

As the chapter has shown, the presentation of the ballads was riddled with contradictions and ambiguity. On the one hand, they were part of an archive of genuine folkloric tradition that gave insight into past beliefs about a supernatural universe; on the other, they were remade to meet market demand for spine-tingling Gothic literature. In handling ballad material in the market for Gothic literature, discerning a clear distinction between the two approaches is not always possible. In addition to the enhancement of terror added to the original ballad material, new satirical versions were included to pre-emptively contain the perceived danger of the irrationalism they possessed. Both serious and self-satirical approaches helped translate folk material into a Gothic idiom, which was a spacious enough container to encompass both.

Chapter 3

THE DANISH WOODS AND
THEIR DEMONS

Deep in the darkest woods, where twisting branches grasp at travellers under cover of night, folklore has long conjured images of malevolent spirits lurking in the shadows. In the eighteenth century, as Romantic ideas began to sprout across Europe, writers became fascinated by exploring the superstition associated with the forest. No one captured this more vividly than Johann Wolfgang von Goethe in the poem 'Erlkönig', an imitation inspired by a Danish ballad Herder translated under the title 'Erlkönigs Tochter'. In this chapter, I will first analyse Goethe's psychological probing of superstition and how the poem's sinister evocation of a wood demon preying on humans inspired later Gothic works. I will then turn to Matthew Lewis' drama *One O'Clock! Or, The Knight and the Wood Dæmon* (1811), which transplanted Goethe's woodland demon to the Danish borderland of Holstein, crafting a spectacle to convey the message that modern rationality can overcome such beliefs. The play was quite popular in its day but has not received as much modern critical attention as Lewis' *The Castle Spectre* (1797).[1] This chapter aims to correct that oversight.

The Erl-King

J. W. Goethe's Danish-inspired ballad 'Erlköning' was first included in the 1782 *Singspiel* entitled *Die Fischerin*. Here, it is sung by the main character, Dortchen, while she patches her father's fishing nets. The play is about the fishing community and their many superstitious beliefs. The ballad's theme of an evil demon in the woods killing humans represents the unsettling notion inherent in Danish ballads that humans are powerless before ancient supernatural forces in nature. The play also features a ballad about a maiden abducted by a merman, sung when Dortchen's father and fiancé believe she has drowned.

---

1 Lewis' play about the Wood Dæmon was later adapted several times. John Turnbull wrote a version for the American provincial theatres in 1808, and there were British adaptations in the 1820s, 1830s and 1840s; see Montague Summers, *A Gothic Bibliography* (Norderstedt: Books on Demand, 2020), 332.

Thus, one may perhaps best see Goethe's ballad as a modern, critical view of superstition and how it determines and misdirects traditional communities. However, something is lost in translation. Herder's rendering of *erl* as a name for the supernatural folkloric creatures, the elves, is a misapprehension of the Danish *Ellefolk*. Herder mistakenly referred to elves as *erl*-people because the Danish word 'elle' can also mean 'alder', which led Goethe to believe the elf-king was specifically a sylvan spirit.

Goethe's ballad is a conversation between a father and his ill boy. The father carries the young child on horseback through a dark forest at a frantic pace, seemingly intent on taking him to a doctor. In the woods, dangers are lurking. In the poem, a third voice is the Erl-King, who appears to speak directly to the boy, tempting him with promises of a better place in his kingdom where his daughter will care for him. Compared to the source material, Goethe amplifies the terror by making the victim a young child. If the seduction is no longer sexual, punishment for refusing an offer made by elves is equally fatal. The last stanza is the intervention of an anonymous narrator who tells us that the boy is dead without revealing whether it is from natural or supernatural causes. Goethe's ballad is a drama of differing perspectives, with multiple voices competing for dominance. It consists of several speech acts: the boy's vision, the father's rejection and the narrator's conclusion. As Geoffrey Hartman puts it, we can either 'accept the supernatural intimation or rationalize it as the product of a fearful or feverish mind'.[2]

The ballad was translated by Matthew Lewis as 'The Erl-King' for *Tales of Wonder* (which is the version quoted in the following). Here, we clearly see how the poem allows for an interpretation in which the boy's fever delirium may be causing him to see and hear things in the forest: 'Oh father! my father! the Erl-King is near! / The Erl-King, with his crown and his beard long and white!'; yet the father is unable to see anything: 'Oh! your eyes are deceived by the vapours of night', and the supernatural creature's whisper is rejected as simply 'the branches, where murmurs the breeze'.[3] In literary terms, it is tempting to propose that the unresolved nature of the boy's vision in Goethe's poem leaves it an open text in ways akin to Tzvetan Todorov's category of 'the fantastic', which marks the reader's final uncertainty about whether a supernatural or rational explanation will prevail.[4]

---

2 Geoffrey Hartman, 'Wordsworth and Goethe in Literary History', *New Literary History* 6, no. 2 (1975): 393–413 (402).
3 *Tales of Wonder*, ed. Matthew Lewis (London: J. Bell, 1801), 55. Henceforth, references to this work will be quoted in brackets within the text as *ToW*.
4 See Tzvetan Todorov, *The Fantastic: A Structural Approach to a Literary Genre* (Ithaca, NY: Cornell University Press, 1975).

In English translation, the ballad appeared at least 47 times before 1860 in various reprints and translations on both sides of the Atlantic.[5] Walter Scott made a translation of the ballad that differs from Lewis' version by explicitly naming the Erl-King a 'Phantom', giving the demon a more ephemeral and ontologically uncertain presence.[6] In this respect, it is worth remembering Shane McCorristine's observation that a 'gradual psychologisation of the ghostly' occurred around the middle of the eighteenth century.[7] That is to say, ghosts and other unexplained phenomena became objects of medical diagnostic models or were considered hallucinations or mistaken perceptions. A culmination of this trend is Scott's *Letters on Demonology and Witchcraft* (1830), a work of scientific anthropology, discussing superstition such as false beliefs in ghosts and witches and attributing such errors of judgement to credulity or 'false impression on the visual nerve'.[8] At several points in his thesis, Scott mentions Norse and Scandinavian influence in establishing the belief in dwarfs, fairies and trolls – for example, the Isle of Man is a 'peculiar depository of the fairy traditions' because it had once been 'conquered by the Norse'.[9] Scott also mentions the Anglo-Saxon belief in the 'man-in-the-oak' as similar to the 'Erl-König of the Germans'.[10]

Lewis came to realise the potential of Goethe's ballad as a modern piece of terror. When he first translated it for publication in 1796, the diction was stilted and consciously old-fashioned to imitate traditional oral balladry.[11] However, the version he includes in *Tales of Wonder*, only a few years later, is written in the kind of uncomplicated prose that would make it read more like a dialogue in a Gothic novel:

'Why trembles my darling? why shrinks he with fear?'
'Oh, father! my father the Erl-King is near!
The Erl-King, with his crown and his beard long and white!'
'Oh! your eyes are deceived by the vapours of night'. (*ToW* 51–52)

---

5 Lucretia Van Tuyl Simmons, *Goethe's Lyric Poems in English Translation Prior to 1800* (Madison: Wisconsin University Studies, 1919), 133–35.

6 Walter Scott, 'The Erl-King', in *Apology for Tales of Terror* (Kelso: Printed at the Mail Office, 1799), 1–3.

7 Shane McCorristine, *Spectres of the Self: Thinking About Ghosts and Ghost-Seeing in England, 1750–1920* (Cambridge: Cambridge University Press, 2010), 32.

8 Walter Scott, *Letters on Demonology and Witchcraft* (London: John Murray, 1830), ii.

9 Ibid., 129.

10 Ibid., 180.

11 Matthew Lewis, 'The Erl-King', *The Monthly Mirror* 2 (October 1796): 371–73.

Perhaps the most ominous element in Lewis' version is the intimate language the Erl-King uses to lure the child: 'Come, baby, sweet baby, with me go away!', which concludes in an eerie euphemism for death: He promises the boy that his daughter 'Shall tend you, and kiss you, and sing you to rest!' (*ToW* 52).

Lewis made it clear in *Tales of Wonder* that Goethe's ballad was 'founded on a Danish tradition' (*ToW* 51), and it thus became a central piece in his construction of elemental beings that ruled over Denmark. However, other British translators sought to clarify the connection to Scandinavian tradition further. The poet and novelist Anna Maria Porter wrote an adaptation entitled 'The Erl; or, Oak King: A Danish Ballad' (1797), in which the young boy walks out in the forest looking for his father but is preyed upon by the Oak-King.[12] This forest demon addresses the boy as 'little Dane' throughout. The terror of the young boy's death is given additional emphasis: 'The forest king he drank his blood –, / His loud cries echo through the wood'.[13] This version is a free adaptation, which includes a lengthy seduction scene utilising the ballad motif of a demon-lover who tricks the innocent female into following him to a happy place. Additionally, the inclusion of the mother's extreme grief over the loss of her son, driving her to try to bring the dead boy back to life, is yet another familiar theme in traditional ballads.

The enthusiastic reception of folk-based ballads in Britain can be considered part of a growing acceptance of folkloric superstition as cultural narratives that could legitimately be used for literary inspiration and present polite readers with images relating to the sublime. Here, it is helpful to turn to one of Joseph Addison's essays, which he published among 11 papers under the general title 'The Pleasures of the Imagination' in the *Spectator*. In this essay from 1712, Addison proposes that immersing oneself in tales of superstition is not only conducive to writing poetry but perhaps also a prerequisite. Addison identifies a tradition linked to the use of 'Fairies, Magicians, Demons, and departed Spirits' in which the nation's greatest writers – Milton, Spenser, and especially Shakespeare – had excelled.[14] Addison argues that only a few classical writers exhibited the audacious quality of 'Darkness and Superstition' in their writing, whereas '[o]ur Forefathers looked upon Nature with more Reverence and Horreur'.[15] Addison goes on to claim that 'the Genius of our

---

12 Anna Maria Porter, 'The Erl; or, Oak King: A Danish Ballad', *The Monthly Visitor, and Entertaining Pocket Companion* (December 1797): 52–57 (52).
13 Ibid., 56.
14 Joseph Addison, *The Spectator*, no. 419 (1 July 1712), vol. 6 (London: S. Buckley and J. Tonson, 1713), 127–31 (127).
15 Ibid. 129.

Country is fitter for this sort of Poetry,' because 'the English are naturally Fanciful, and very often disposed by that Gloominess and wild Melancholy of Temper, which is so frequent in our Nation, to many wild Notions and Visions, to which others are not so liable'.[16] Yvonne Bezrucka has seen Addison's essay as indicative of a broader impulse in eighteenth-century British literary history to argue for an autochthonous tradition of a particular 'Northern Aesthetics'.[17]

To illustrate the ability of Germanic folklore to create an elevated sublime, we see attempts to connect the ballads Goethe bases his poem on with ancient mythology. The Norwich scholar William Taylor's translation from 1798 is one example. His version makes it clear that we are to understand that the boy freezes to death. In the headnote, Taylor explains that 'those frozen to death' were supposed to have been seized by 'the Deuses of Frost', also known as *Hrimthurs* in the Edda, and that it was 'a remnant of this superstition' that appears to have inspired the ballad.[18] Therefore, the demon lures the boy with the promise of a happy garden that will remain green '[a]ll winter in spite of the cold'.[19] Taylor retitles the ballad 'King of the Deuses', claiming that the 'Erlkönig' can be seen as a fallen frost giant. In other words, he reconstitutes the ballad as a reflection of the 'Giants of the Frost', described in Paul-Henri Mallet's work on the Norse tradition as creatures belonging to the mythology of 'the Gothic nations'.[20] The idea that the folklore of the fairies and elves reflected fragments of more ancient religious imagining was later addressed by the critic Nathan Drake, who explained Shakespeare's reduction of the mythological Norns to three witches in *Macbeth* as the 'vulgar Gothic', an epithet he adopts 'to distinguish the lowly Germanic superstition from 'the regular mythology of the Edda'.[21]

---

16 Ibid. 129–30.

17 Yvonne Bezrucka, *The Invention of Northern Aesthetics in 18th-Century English Literature* (Newcastle upon Tyne: Cambridge Scholars Publishing, 2017), esp. 27–80.

18 William Taylor, 'Ballad from the Original of J. W. von Goethe', *The Monthly Magazine* 6 (September 1798): 197. Lewis included Taylor's version of Bürger's 'Lenore' in *Tales of Wonder*. For a discussion of this poem and other English versions, see Robert W. Rix, 'The Elf-King: Translation, Transmission, and Transfiguration', in *Nordic Romanticism: Translation, Transmission, Transformation*, ed. Cian Duffy and Robert W. Rix (Cham: Palgrave, 2022), 1–30.

19 Ibid.

20 Paul-Henri Mallet, *Northern Antiquities: or, a Description of the Manners, Customs, Religion and Laws of the Ancient Danes, and Other Northern Nations; Including Those of Our Own Saxon Ancestors*, trans. Thomas Percy, vol. 2 (London: T. Carnan and Co., 1770), 10.

21 Nathan Drake, *Literary Hours: Or, Sketches Critical and Narrative* (London: T. Cadell, 1798), 88.

By establishing connections between the folk traditions of the Germanic people and its ancient mythological roots, Taylor seemed to have hoped to signify how grand and sublime images were woven into the cultural fabric and psychology of the race. Tracing folklore, usually associated with the lower classes, to ancient mythology was re-making folklore as symbolic capital that could rival classical poetry in its sublime imagery. In his *Historic Survey of German Poetry* (1828–30), Taylor includes a long section about the Edda, how it belongs to the early beginning of Northern nations, and how it was 'successively imitated by Danes, Englanders, Norwegians, Swedes, and Icelanders and have formed collectively a northern school of poetic fiction'.[22] The Edda, Taylor claims, sparked an 'original school of poetry not inferior to the Greek'.[23] Among later nineteenth-century English folklorists, we also see the national importance of elaborating the connections between lowly folklore (previously roundly disregarded as trash) with the sublime mythology of ancient to enhance the reputation of English tradition.[24]

The reorientation of Goethe's imitation of a folklore ballad, claiming that the imagery can be traced to Eddic mythology, is a shift in perspective that transforms the ballad's status as terror writing. When connected with the mythology of ancient giants, the ballad's imagery evokes a sense of metaphysical dread than the terrors usually associated with lowly folklore. It brings about a more pronounced feeling of existential dread, as it emphasises the powerlessness of humans in a cosmos dominated by mysterious and malevolent entities. This terror challenges the belief that humans are of utmost importance in the order of existence. This idea of vast, ancient supernatural forces controlling the universe can perhaps be compared to the self-invented mythology of cosmic horror that the American writer H. P. Lovecraft developed in his stories from the early twentieth century. As Lovecraft himself would acknowledge, 'the Scandinavian Eddas and Sagas thunder with cosmic horror'.[25]

The idea that ballad folklore could retain elements of original mythology was also proposed in an 1833 edition of the Boston-based *The New-England Magazine*. Here, a translation of Goethe's poem, entitled 'The Wood Demon',

---

22 William Taylor, *Historic Survey of German Poetry: Interspersed with Various Translations*, Volume 1 (London: Treutel et al., 1830), 32.

23 Ibid., 30.

24 See Jonathan Roper, 'England – The Land without Folklore?', in *Folklore and Nationalism in Europe During the Long Nineteenth Century*, ed. Timothy Baycroft and David Hopkin (Boston: Brill, 2012), 227–54.

25 H. P. Lovecraft, *Supernatural Horror in Literature* (Abergele: Wermod and Wermod Publishing Group, 2013), 15.

is printed with a headnote proposing that the evil sprite is descended from the frost giants of Norse mythology. According to the anonymous translator, the Anglo-American folklore of 'Jack Frost', who personifies the winter cold, is 'a lineal descendant' from this mythological layer of ancient Germanic culture.[26] A similar idea is elaborated in the German writer Heinrich Heine's essay *Elementargeister* [Elemental spirits] (1834), in which he proposes the theory that pagan gods of old had gone into 'exile' and now appear as folkloristic fairies and elves in folklore. In the essay, he paraphrases the Danish elf ballads.[27]

Staging the Demonic

After examining how Germanic folklore was a source of both cultural preservation and inspiration for terror poetry, I will now turn attention to the domain of theatre, where Matthew Lewis breathed new life into the evil spirit of the woods. Lewis wrote several manuscripts for the stage, and his drama *The Wood Daemon; Or, 'The Clock Has Struck!* premiered at Drury Lane on 1 April 1807. In contrast to Goethe's approach of maintaining uncertainty about the reality of the demonic presence in nature, Lewis immerses himself in the possibilities the Gothic theatre offers and indulges his supernatural imagination. Hence, the character is allowed to appear in physical form and actively direct the unfolding action.

In *The Monk*, Lewis had already prepared an understanding of the Erl-King as a regal figure, with crown and accoutrements, who practically holds the land of Denmark to ransom with his evil spell. In Theodore's account:

> The Woods are haunted by a malignant power, called 'The Erl, or Oak King:' he it is who blights the Trees, spoils the Harvest, and commands the Imps and Goblins. He appears in the form of an old Man of majestic figure with a golden Crown, and long white beard. His principal amusement is to entice young Children from their Parents, and as soon as He gets them into his Cave, He tears them into a thousand pieces.[28]

In *The Wood Daemon*, Lewis transforms this scenario into a tale of actual political power by letting the daemon exert control over the Duke of Holstein. The tale is a Faustian story (Goethe published his famous *Faust. Eine Tragödie*, only a year later, in 1808), in which a deal involving the sacrifice of children

---

26 'The Wood Demon', *The New-England Magazine* (July 1833): 7.
27 For an English translation, see 'Elementary Spirits', in *The Works of Heinrich Heine*, vol. 6, trans. Charles Godfrey Leland (London: William Heinemann, 1892), 110–211 (130–38).
28 Matthew Lewis, *The Monk*, vol. 3 (London: J. Bell, 1796), 14–15.

is struck with the daemon of the forest. The reward is dominance over Holstein.

It is fitting that Goethe's popular figure of the wood daemon was used in a Gothic drama, as this rose to become a very popular medium in Georgian Britain. Matthew Lewis' drama *The Wood Daemon* (1807) was revised for performance, premiering on 1 August 1811 at the Lyceum under the new title *One O'Clock! Or, The Knight and the Wood Dæmon*, described as 'A Grand Musical Romance with choruses and several ballads'.[29] It is the published version of this later play that will be analysed in the following. The imagery of an evil wood spirit is partly a version of the 'Erl-King, who haunts the forest and abducts children. We are given no backstory about her in the play except that she comes from 'Far in the North'.[30] The wood daemon is called Sangrida, a name borrowed from Thomas Gray's poem 'The Fatal Sisters', in which she is listed as one of the Valkyries deciding the fate of men. Indeed, Sangrida reigns over the fates and lives of humans in the play.

Cultural historians examining Gothic stage plays often emphasise the visual effects of elaborate sets, spectacular violence and striking props.[31] The first appearance of Sangrida in a black cloud with her entourage is an attempt to make her a menacing figure of the sublime. She is the 'awful Mistress', to whom minor wood spirits 'bend the knee'.[32] She emerges on stage in a carriage drawn by two mechanical dragons created by Alexander Johnson, who was a talented machinist.[33] This procession was the play's major theatrical spectacle. As the *Monthly Mirror* wrote, 'The confusion and apparent horror which ensued after the appearance of the spectre combined to form perhaps the most terrific and sublime scene ever to behold on the stage'.[34]

The evil spirit is here a queen of the forest, rather than a king, which may be Lewis' attempt to make the plot fit with the idea that a female lures a peasant to gain wealth and power, as in the Danish elf ballads. In 'Elver's Hoh', for

---

29 Matthew Lewis, *One O'Clock! or, the Knight and the Wood Dæmon. A Grand Musical Romance* (London: Lowndes and Hobbs, 1811).

30 Lewis, *One O'Clock!*, 6.

31 See Michael Gamer, 'Gothic Melodrama', in *The Cambridge Companion to English Melodrama*, ed. Carolyn Williams (Cambridge: Cambridge University Press, 2018), 31–46.

32 Lewis, *One O'Clock!*, 7.

33 Ibid.

34 Quoted in Jeffrey M. Cox, 'Gothic Drama: Tragedy or Comedy', in *The Oxford Handbook of the Georgian Theatre 1737–1832*, ed. Julia Swindells and David Francis Taylor (Oxford: Oxford University Press, 2014), 407–23 (416).

example, the knight is lured by the promise of 'the sorcerer's treasure' (*ToW* 32). Changing the Erl-King to a woman also seems less drastic when we know, from the list of *dramatis personae*, that the role of Sangrida was played by a man ('Mr Robert'). The gender confusion undoubtedly has significance in terms of placing emphasis on the illicit attraction Hardyknute has to the daemon, not unlike Ambrosio's attraction to the young boy Rosario, who turns out to be Matilda, in *The Monk*. However, I will focus on the Scandinavian lore that forms the background for Lewis' play and the reflection on illicit political power as something connected with irrationality and superstition.

Before the play is discussed in detail, it is useful to give a short summary. Hardyknute is a 'peasant', who was 'trampled on' by both poor and rich, and born with physical deformities, which made him full of 'Pride, Passion, and Vengeance'.[35] To gain power, eternal youth, and great physical beauty, he makes a Faustian pact with Sangrida, an evil spirit of the forest. The terms of this unholy agreement stipulate an annual ritual involving the sacrifice of a child to Sangrida before 1 a.m. on 7 August. Failure to fulfil this obligation will condemn Hardyknute to become the daemon's prey. We learn that Hardyknute's sacrifice will be the ninth of its kind. The idea of human sacrifice to purchase divine favour was associated with the religion of Odin. For example, Joseph Cottle, in a note to his long poem *Alfred* (1800), notes that 'Hacon, king of Norway, offered his son in sacrifice to obtain of Odin the victory over his enemy Harold' and that 'Aune, king of Sweden, devoted to Odin the blood of his nine sons, to prevail on that god to prolong his life'.[36] In the notes, Cottle expands on the importance of the number nine to the Danes in the context of sacrifice, which may be a tradition also reflected in Lewis' play.

Meanwhile, Leolyn, a mute boy, unknowingly holds the legitimate claim to Holstein as the son of Ruric, Count of Holstein, whom Hardyknute has murdered. However, he does not know this, as his mother has hidden him from the murderer to avoid danger. In an allusion to another Danish setting, Shakespeare's *Hamlet*, Hardyknute is left deeply disturbed by a play-within-a-play: a ballet is performed for him in which Leolyn has a role. Hardyknute notices the boy's likeness to the old Count and cuts the performance short. The usurper becomes convinced of Leolyn's rightful claim to Holstein through the tell-tale mark of a bloodstained arrow on the boy's wrist. This makes Hardyknute determined to give the boy to Sangrida as the ninth human offering. Leolyn's protector is Una, an exquisite young lady whom Hardyknute

---

35 Ibid., 76.
36 Joseph Cottle, *Alfred. An Epic Poem* (London: Longman and Rees, 1800), 235.

has rescued from the giant Hacho (a name borrowed from the Norse poem 'King Hacho's Death Song', which Lewis had translated in *Tales of Wonder*). Hardyknute has subsequently enchanted Una to desert her lover, Oswy, and marry him instead. When Una exposes Hardyknute's devilish deal with the wood daemon, he apprehends her and decides to sacrifice her instead of the boy in his underground cavern. However, in a critical moment, Leolyn manages to advance the hand of the clock to the fateful hour. Sangrida materialises, and with no boy in sight, she seizes Hardyknute and stabs him, after which four demon fiends drag him to an alter and sacrifice him. In the supernatural denouement of the play, the earth yawns open as the wood daemon drags Hardyknute into the depths of Hell. Subsequently, with the usurper having received his comeuppance, Leolyn is greeted as the new rightful Lord of Holstein.

In Lewis' drama, a sorceress transforms the deformed Hardyknute into 'the handsomest Knight in all Europe'.[37] This is done not with the help of the Devil, as in the Faustian tradition, but by interventions of a Germanic supernatural figure. It is interesting to compare this spellbinding plot with Thomas John Dibdin's pantomime *Harlequin's Magnet; Or, Scandinavian Sorcerer* (first performed at Theatre Royal, Covent Garden, 30 December 1805). In this play, the evil Northern sorcerer Nor, assisted by the mistress of the underworld (Hela), enchants the beautiful princess Fylla with a magical magnet. However, Fylla's true love, the youth Harald, is assisted by Odin, who grants him the powers of Harlequin, a traditional trickster character in the theatre. The play concludes with Fylla and Harald winning each other's hands.[38]

As a Gothic figure tempted by evil powers, Hardyknute is a familiar character. Like Shakespeare's Richard III, his original deformity is a sign of his inherent villainy, which becomes concealed through the transformation he undergoes as a result of his demonic deal. The wood daemon is a pagan or pre-Christian reference that replaces the Catholic Devil, who has a hold on Ambrosio's soul in *The Monk*. But more than just sexual desire and psychological power over others, which are themes in *The Monk*, Lewis' drama explores the issues of ambition and temptation and the consequences of pursuing a passion for political power.

---

37 Lewis, *One O'Clock!*, 15. In the 'Advertisement' to the printed play, Lewis states that the theme of the deformity is taken from *Joshua Pickersgill Jr'.s Gothic romance, The Three Brothers* (1803).

38 Thomas John Dibdin, 'Harlequin's Magnet; or, Scandinavian Sorcerer', manuscript in the Huntington Library, https://www.eighteenthcenturydrama.amdigital.co.uk/Documents/Details/HL_LA_mssLA1468.

Robert Miles reminds us that the themes of what constitutes proper rule and authority are integral to how the Gothic was perceived and consumed.[39] In *One O'Clock!*, the relationship between supernatural and political power can be construed specifically as a metaphor for the enigmatic nature of politics, which was often associated with deception and trickery. Other earlier plays had reflected this idea. We see this in, for example, the political reformer and poet John Thelwall's drama *The Fairy of the Lake* (1801). Here, the Saxon sorceress Rowenna is described as the 'pride of Woden's race' and 'chauntress of the Runic song', and she attributes her political power over the native Britons to her 'minstrelsy and voice, / Obedient to my wishes'.[40] Thelwall explains in an appendix that he conceived the figure based on 'Northern Mythology' and quotes Mallet's historical work.[41] In *One O'Clock!*, Lewis also associates dark magic with the wielding of political power, however without the radical implications of Thelwall's play. Lewis' insistence on punishing a usurper who does not respect the rightfulness of primogeniture embodies what James Watt refers to as the 'loyalist Gothic', a category in which we find Horace Walpole's *The Castle of Otranto* (1764) and Clara Reeve's *The Old English Baron* (1778) as early examples.[42] As Paula Backscheider analyses Gothic drama, it emerges as a mode of representation at a time of crisis in Britain, for which reason it solidifies into a form that invests art with the ideological function of strengthening the political status quo.[43]

Lewis' drama does not offer political commentary with a readily decodable meaning. Nonetheless, the setting in Holstein (now northern Germany) would have evoked a nexus of ideas for theatregoers at the time. Holstein combined an association with both Germany and Denmark – the two prominent spaces for Gothic terror. Holstein was a duchy with the Holy Roman Empire, yet it was ruled by the Danish king, as it was in personal union with Denmark (and it remained so until the war of 1864).[44] In the chapbook version, which converts the play into prose, the first line is quite simply: 'Many centuries ago, on the proud shores

---

39 For a helpful discussion, see Robert Miles, 'Political Gothic Fiction', in *Romantic Gothic: An Edinburgh Companion*, ed. Angela Wright and Dale Townshend (Edinburgh: Edinburgh University Press, 2015), 129–46.

40 John Thelwall, *Poems Chiefly Written in Retirement* (London: W. H. Parker, 1801), 5.

41 Ibid., 203.

42 James Watt, *Contesting the Gothic: Fiction, Genre, and Cultural Conflict, 1764–1832* (Cambridge: Cambridge University Press, 1999), 42–69.

43 Paula Backscheider, *Spectacular Politics: Theatrical Power and Mass Culture in Early Modern England* (Baltimore: Johns Hopkins University Press, 1993), 149–233.

44 It is mentioned in the play that the evil Count of Holstein has the King of Denmark as his 'feudal Sovereign' and 'Liege Lord'. See Lewis, *One O'Clock!*, 16, 70.

of Denmark, stood the majestic towers of Holstein castle'.[45] In terms of connections with Germanic lore, Holstein was also a name associated with a superstition about trees. This was especially the magic of the mistletoe which grows on oak, as readers of Mallet's work would have known.[46] The mistletoe appears as a central object in the Edda in connection with the story of the god Baldr. This is a narrative of deception committed by Loki, the mischievous god, who uses the magic of the mistletoe to kill Baldr. This ancient tale of magic trickery fittingly provides a thematic backdrop for Lewis' stage play with its own themes of magic disguise and clandestine scheming.

Lewis depicts Holstein as an isolated, peripheral region. Thus, when Hardyknute's foul play is discovered, the characters speak of having to journey to Copenhagen to alert the Danish king.[47] The concept of Holstein as a remote location far from the centre would have been well suited as a locale where folklore demons could exert their evil power. For Lewis, Holstein becomes a liminal space suspended between different political alliances, making it a prime location for a narrative about a usurper who carves out a space of local power for himself. However, when the play premiered at Drury Lane on 1 April 1807, Holstein acquired political importance in relation to the ongoing conflict with Napoleonic France, irrespective of Lewis' original intent. In early November 1806, a French task force entered Holstein to engage a Prussian detachment, leading to a skirmish with Danish frontier troops. The Danish Prince protested to the French commander but later ordered Danish forces to withdraw. Although Denmark claimed this was not due to French pressure, it did seem to align with French interests, as Napoleon did not want a Danish army near his lines during his Polish campaign. Britain was concerned about Danish withdrawal from Holstein, which was seen as practically ceding territory. In one of the periodicals at the time, a letter writer weighed in on the situation: 'I have no longer any hesitation in pronouncing that he [the Danish king] was the determined partizan of Bonaparte and meant to aid his designs against this country' because when Bonaparte took 'possession of Holstein', he was able to make a 'Northern confederacy carry the vengeance of Europe to the shores of Great Britain'.[48]

---

45 *One O'Clock; or, the Knight and the Wood Demon. Founded on the popular piece, of that name, as performed at the Theatres' Royal* (London: G. Drake, c. 1840), 239.

46 Mallet, *Northern Antiquities*, 2:143 note.

47 Lewis, *One O'Clock!*, 60.

48 'Letter to the Editor: Vindication of the War against Denmark', *Flower's Political Review and Monthly Register* (November 1807): 314–17 (317).

The Danish failure to take a firm stance against Napoleon eventually led to the British bombardment of Copenhagen (16 August–7 September 1807) to capture or destroy the Danish fleet, so the French could not use it.[49]

As George Taylor notes, London theatre audiences clamoured for stories about power, social change and political intrigue, but plays delivered this mainly in the guise of plots that were 'loosely metaphorical rather than strictly allegorical'.[50] This would also apply to Lewis' drama. However, Rachael Pearson suggests, albeit only in passing, that Hardyknute, who had risen to power and magically rendered 'invulnerable in battle', could be a refraction of the legend of Napoleon that was developing during those years.[51] This suggestion deserves a hearing. Developments concerning Holstein could hardly have escaped audiences' attention. The fact is that Lewis did not keep his antagonism against Napoleonic France out of the theatre. When Napoleon entered Madrid, the commander of the British forces in Spain, Sir John Moore, was killed. Lewis wrote a monody praising him, which was recited at Drury Lane Theatre by Mrs Powell in early 1809. Lewis here warns: 'A day shall come at length (a day of dread) / When France shall wish the hero's blood unshed'.[52]

One O'Clock! is manifestly about illegitimate power based on political and military might. Hardyknute has, through his pact with the wood daemon, seen military successes, including saving the Danish king on the battlefield and slaying the giant Hacho. Critics were aware that supernatural beings could be distorted representations of actual political figures. The literary antiquarian Richard Hurd, for example, suggested that the ogres of Germanic legend may be symbolic representations of the monsters of the social world. He famously made the claim that the 'Giants' of medieval romances were, in fact, imaginative transformations of 'oppressive feudal Lords', who are 'shadowed out' in the old tales as monstrous.[53]

At the time Lewis was writing, society's bugbears were also 'Gothicised' in this manner. In *One O'Clock!*, the sacrifice of a child for political power

---

49 Gareth Glover, *The Two Battles of Copenhagen, 1801 And 1807: Britain and Denmark in the Napoleonic Wars* (Barnsley: Pen & Sword Books, 2018), 104–109.

50 George Taylor, *The French Revolution and the London Stage, 1789–1805* (Cambridge: Cambridge University Press, 2001), 29.

51 Rachael Pearson, 'Politics and Power in the Gothic Drama of M. G. Lewis', PhD thesis, University of Southampton, 2011, p. 244. Citation in Lewis, *One O'Clock!*, 76.

52 'Monody on the Death of Sir John Moore', in Margaret Baron-Wilson, *The Life and Correspondence of M.G. Lewis*, vol. 1 (London: Henry Colburn, 1839), 380.

53 Richard Hurd, *Letters on Chivalry and Romance* (London: A. Millar, W. Thurlbourn, and J. Woodyer, 1762), 28.

hits home with the propaganda of scaremongering that was sometimes used against enemies. A nursery rhyme about Napoleon as a cannibalistic monster is recorded in various versions from the early years of his military campaigns:

> And he breakfasts, dines, rely on't,
> Every day on naughty people.
> [...] And he'll eat you, eat you, eat you,
> Every morsel, snap, snap, snap![54]

Another context in which Napoleon is demonised is Henry Boyd's 1805 poem 'The Witch of Lapland. In Imitation of Gray's Descent of Odin. Written after the Storm that scattered the English Fleet off Brest January 1803'. The passage portrays Napoleon as a horrifying figure, referred to as 'the fiend of Gaul' and a 'Demon'. He is shown descending into a Lapland cave to make a deal with a witch. In exchange for her help creating a storm that will disrupt the British navy blockade, Napoleon offers her the burning of towns and jewels taken from European crowns.[55]

Politics and demonic deals are also intertwined in Lewis' play. Holstein is a far-away duchy where a power grab may easily take place. When Hardyknute's usurpation is finally exposed, Una's lover, Oswy, is about to go to Copenhagen to convey the truth to the King of Denmark. However, Oswy fears his absence will lead to Hardyknute further bolstering his illegitimate power base by taking Una as his wife.[56] If punishment in the drama is finally served up by the wood daemon, rather than the legal judiciary system, true justice for Hardyknute is secured by the ingenuity of the true heir to Holstein, Leolyn, with the help of Una. They play a final trick on Hardyknute by manipulating the hands of the grand clock to turn the schemer's scheme against him. By fast-forwarding the clock to one, Sangrida appears and snatches Hardyknute as her prey before he can prepare a victim for her. In this way, justice is meted out by a moral universe. The conclusion is in line with Gothic texts generally and Lewis' versions of these in particular: those who fail to control their desire will (literally) be destroyed as a consequence of their inability to resist temptation.

---

54 Cited in Carolyn Daniel, *Voracious Children: Who Eats Whom in Children's Literature* (New York: Routledge, 2006), 151.

55 The poem was originally printed as an addendum to Henry Boyd's translation of Vincenzo Monti's *The Penance of Hugo, A Vision on the French Revolution* (1805) but was reprinted and excerpted in several periodicals. See, for example, *The Annual Register* (1806): 905–907.

56 Lewis, *One O'Clock!*, 71.

The fact that Hardyknute is a low-born man who gains power through a deal with demonic forces carries a significant message. It reinforces the conservative ideology that wrongful seizure of state power is detrimental to society. Lewis exposes folklore demons as holding only illegitimate authority. Their enticement of humans into self-destruction through promises of wealth and power aligns with the parallel notion that a peasant may successfully ascend to the helm of the state. For all its special effects and exploitative terror, the play speaks to the upholding of primogeniture, inherited power and social order – values essentially imperilled by the threat of revolution or the fear of Napoleonic rule imposed upon Europe. As a way of highlighting the patriotic values of the play, Lewis dedicated the printed version to Princess Charlotte Augusta of Wales, the only child of George IV and Caroline of Brunswick.[57] Charlotte August was expected to ascend the British throne but died during childbirth on 6 November 1817, before her father.

Lewis' play can be interpreted as a rejection of Scandinavian superstition, where a sacrifice was necessary to appease demonic supernatural beings as part of the old world's ritual time. With the actions of Una and Leolyn, who manipulate the large clock on the stage in the final scene, a new era is ushered in. This is done by forwarding the clock's hands to a time when the old world's power becomes the past. The future is a happy vision where the devilish deal that has cost the lives of Holstein's children is rendered obsolete, and illegitimate rule comes to an end. Frederick Burwick has given a long and illuminating account of the importance of time in Lewis' *One O'Clock!*.[58] However, he does not link the manipulation of technology in the play with the British pride in technological advancement as the nation's pride. Nonetheless, I would argue that this is an essential part of the meaning of the timepiece in Lewis' play. Like the young woman in Lewis' 'The Cloud-King' who triumphs over the ancient Scandinavian fiend by dint of her modern education in grammar, the young woman Una in *One O'Clock!* emerges victorious by employing her understanding of technology to defeat Hardyknute. He is rendered outdated, as he literally runs out of clock time. As Lewis Mumford once commented, 'the clock, not the steam-engine, is the key machine of the modern age'.[59] British chronometry was essential for upholding the empire, and the export of timepieces was booming; the world was buying British time.[60] The ability to

---

57 'Advertisement' (signed 21 August 1811), in ibid.
58 Frederick Burwick, *Time in Romantic Theatre* (Cham: Palgrave, 2022), 82–86.
59 Lewis Mumford, *Technics and Civilization* (1934; Chicago, IL: University of Chicago Press, 2010), 14.
60 See Mary A. Favret, *War at a Distance: Romanticism and the Making of Modern Wartime* (Princeton, NJ: Princeton University Press, 2009), 44–53.

manipulate clock technology symbolically ticks the old world out of existence, resigning Hardyknute and his Scandinavian demon to the past.

Conclusion

In this chapter, we have seen how Goethe's 'Erlkönig' took on a life of its own in British adaptations. Inspired by Danish ballads, the poem became a vehicle for exploring a deeper connection with a cultural memory of Norse mythology and the evil forces it posited as ruling the world. In his play *One O'Clock!*, Lewis elevated the figure of the wood daemon to serve in a theatrical spectacle, where the diabolical power no longer only poses a threat to life but also challenges the very foundations of political order by allowing a usurper to assume power. It is pertinent here to revisit the choice of Holstein as a location where folkloric supernaturalism is allowed to reign. Officially a dukedom under the Danish king, it became a place of political significance during the Napoleonic Wars. Also relevant to what the broad public would have associated with Holstein was its designation as an ethnic homeland of the English. To give just one example, the historian Robert Henry writes: 'The chief seat of the people properly called Saxons was in [...] Holstein [...] several bands of Saxon adventurers came over and fixed themselves in Britain where their posterity still flourish'.[61] Thus, Lewis also makes the drama a warning about British politics at a time when the social status quo and the ruling order were regularly challenged, or at least conservative observers believed social order needed to be defended.

Goethe's poem about the evil spirit in the woods leaves readers' interpretation suspended between ascribing events to supernatural forces or a mind overheated by superstition. There is no such ambiguity in Lewis' play, in which the wood spirit is tangible and physically present, existing within the world of the drama. However, the dramatic narrative is a drive away from the supernatural. The daemon and her magic that keeps Hardyknute at the helm are finally driven out, giving way to the establishment of a legitimate, non-supernatural rule that promises the restoration of order and societal harmony. Diane Long Hoeveler has described melodrama as emerging from the traditional worldview of transcendent cosmic order and embracing a new consciousness of the bourgeois individual who triumphs through self-assertion.[62] In *One O'Clock!*, the plot follows such a trajectory as Una and

---

61 Robert Henry, *The History of Great Britain*, vol. 3 (London: T. Cadell, and W. Davies, 1805), 304. Cf. Mallet, *Northern Antiquities*, 1:21.
62 Diane Long Hoeveler, 'The Temple of Morality: Thomas Holcroft and the Swerve of Melodrama', *European Romantic Review* 14, no. 1 (2003): 49–63 (53).

Leolyn triumph over the supernatural agents by deploying rational thinking. This approach enables them to overcome the old world dominated by supernatural beliefs. In sum, both Goethe's poem and Lewis' play captivated audiences by skilfully incorporating Scandinavian folklore superstitions into their creative endeavours. However, they each challenge these beliefs in their own way, pointing out their fallacy and encouraging their audiences to look beyond them.

Chapter 4

SCANDINAVIAN BRITAIN

This chapter excavates the revisionary literary imaginings of Britain's Danish settlers and its former pagan religion of Odin. One mainstream view of the Viking attackers on churches and Anglo-Saxon kingdoms is epitomised in the Oxford antiquarian Francis Wise's comment from the 1750s that 'the Danes perpetuated such a scene of villainy as is scarce to be parallel'd in the stories of the most savage nations'.[1] In texts published in the late eighteenth and early nineteenth centuries, several authors sought to reposition the Scandinavian element of British history. Through an analysis of select works by Wordsworth, Walter Scott and Ann Radcliffe, the chapter reveals how specific texts generated imaginative spaces to rethink and recontextualise the inheritances left by Scandinavian interlopers and settlers. The central contention is that authors presented the old antagonists in new guises as part of a historical trajectory, forging a more inclusive conception of British national identity. Through readings and contextualisation of key texts, I will demonstrate how fictional characters of Scandinavian origin come to symbolise Britain's progression towards social cohesion and a shared Christian faith. In other words, we find a recognition of the role of the ancient Danes in shaping the modern nation.

Revisiting Britain's 'Others'

Against the backdrop of war and unrest in the 1790s, the spectre of past atrocities committed against the Danes is reflected in an often overlooked poem by William Wordsworth, first published in *Lyrical Ballads* (1800) entitled 'A Fragment' (later retitled 'The Danish Boy. A Fragment'). The poem is a vignette of a ghost, a Danish boy, whose singing can sometimes be heard in a moorland dell. He can be seen as a 'Spirit of noon-day', almost like 'a form of flesh and blood', dressed in his 'regal vest of fur [...] In colour like

---

1 Cited in Rosemary Sweet, *Antiquaries: The Discovery of the Past in Eighteenth-Century Britain* (London: Hambledon, 2004), 220.

a raven's wing'.[2] As Wordsworth would later recall, the stanzas were initially meant 'to introduce a Ballad upon the Story of a Danish Prince who had fled from Battle, and, for the sake of the valuables about him, was murdered by the Inhabitant of a Cottage in which he had taken refuge'.[3] The killing of a prince who had deliberately abandoned war is an injustice, and this seems to explain why he has become a ghost haunting the landscape. If there is initially an eeriness about the ghostly scene, we learn that his thoughts are not on 'bloody deeds'.[4] The text thus offers a subversion of Gothic paradigms by introducing a spectre that is essentially a benevolent presence. The intention to live peacefully on English soil, which he was denied in life, is now made possible as he has become an organic part of the British landscape. The non-threatening ghost becomes a figure of imaginative healing of past conflict. The murder of the Dane symbolises a cultural memory of past violence that casts a solemn shadow over British history. Rejecting the prevalent practice of locating an oppositional 'Other' as the sole origin of social ills and violence, the poem places responsibility for wrongs onto the English themselves. The ghostly presence vocalises from beyond the grave the underrepresented yet integral role the Danish heritage plays in Cumbria. Thomas De Quincey made precisely this point when he traced the dialects of Lake country to the Danish language, even asserting an 'ultra-Danish influence' in Windermere.[5] Wordsworth's re-conceptualisation of a Danish ghost was enough of a radical departure from the usual idea of Danish violence that the *British Quarterly Review* would comment that this ghost story is 'so free from every element of terror' that 'We can scarcely believe that such a graceful superstition was brought from Scandinavia'.[6] It was not, of course; it was Wordsworth's own fancy, reminding the present to avoid repeating violent actions and instead embrace a conception of community.

In terms of revisionary depictions of the Danish invaders through a Gothic lens, one of the most interesting works is Walter Scott's verse narrative *Harold the Dauntless* (1817).[7] Here, we have a Danish warrior who converts

---

2 William Wordsworth, *Lyrical Ballads, with Other Poems*, 2 vols. (London: T. N. Longman and O. Rees, 1800), 2:172.

3 William Wordsworth, *The Poetical Works*, vol. 2 (London: Longman, Rees, Orme, Brown and Green, 1827), 352.

4 Wordsworth, *Lyrical Ballads*, 2:174.

5 Thomas De Quincey, 'The Lake Dialect', *Titan* (January 1757): 89–92 (92).

6 Review of E. Lynn Linton's *The Lake Country*, in *British Quarterly Review* (April 1865): 476–95 (489).

7 Walter Scott, *Harold the Dauntless. A Poem in Six Cantos* (London: Longman, Hurst, Rees, Orme and Brown, 1817).

to Christianity. As a result, the former berserker becomes integrated into an emerging Britain that leaves past conflicts behind to progress towards a more civilised national identity. Scott possessed the requisite scholarship to write a poem about Scandinavian Britain. He was an avid student of Norse heroic literature. In 1801, he considered a publication project that would be 'an abridgement of the most celebrated Sagas, selecting the most picturesque Incidents & translating the Runic Rhymes'.[8] He abandoned the project but would later produce a paraphrase of the Icelandic *Eyrbyggja saga* for the collection *Illustrations of Northern Antiquities* (1814).

Harold the Dauntless is a saga-like poem in six cantos, in which Scott mines the Norse tradition to create supernatural events and images of terror. The poem concerns the Viking Harold, whose family settled in Northumbria (part of the areas of the Danelaw) following the Viking incursion of York in 866. Harold's father, Count Witikind, receives church land near Durham in exchange for accepting a Christian baptism. Harold declines to forsake the Norse faith of his ancestors and leaves home in disgust, accompanied by his loyal page, Gunnar. During his perilous journey across the shadowy English plains, Harold meets Jutta, a witch who worships the East-European god Zernebrock, whom she summons to learn about Harold's marriage proposal to her daughter, Metelill. Canto II unfolds a Gothic tableau in which Jutta's 'necromantic words and charms' wake the deity from his otherworldly slumber. Yet, despite the resonant echoes of the deity's deep voice, Jutta gains no revelatory insights into the matter. After Witikind's death, the church authorities conspire to dispossess Harold of his father's land. For him to regain control, the clergy demand that Harold prove his bravery by spending a night in the enchanted Castle of the Seven Shields. On the night of his endeavour, Harold encounters his father Witikind's apparition, who tells him he is condemned to wander the earth until his son repents his pagan ways. Harold adopts Christianity, and as a converted berserker he reaches the castle. Here, Harold confronts the spirit of Odin in 'living form'.[9] Odin tempts Harold with promises of drinking mead from skulls in Vahalla if he reverts to the old ways. But Harold refuses. In the ensuing battle, Harold defeats the evil spirit and saves Gunnar, to whom Odin lays claim. Defeating Odin is a symbolic rejection of 'Evil power / Adored by all his [Harold's] race'.[10] Gunnar is revealed to be Eivir, a (Christian) Danish maiden in disguise. Harold receives his baptism and marries Eivir on the same morning.

---

8 Letter dated 27 March 1801 to George Ellis, in *The Letters of Sir Walter Scott*, ed. Herbert Grierson, vol. 12 (London: Constable, 1932–1937), 178.
9 Scott, *Harold*, 189.
10 Ibid.

In the poem, Scott conceives of a character similar to the eponymous rebel in his novel *Rob Roy*, which was also published in 1817. Both anti-heroes are described as rugged and dirty defenders of a dying culture. However, whereas the novel ends with Rob Roy supporting the Jacobite rebellion, which is a dead end in British history, Harold converts to Christianity, which will shape Britain's future. Harold is a morally redeemable character who symbolises a Britain forged out of tensions that resolve conflicts across ethnic and religious boundaries. In depicting the defeat of Odin, Scott has, in the most allegorical of fashions, dramatised the end of Norse Britain. Yet, in his standoff with Odin, Harold successfully defeats this evil spirit by combining 'his new-born faith' with 'some tokens of his ancient mood'.[11] Despite the transformative shift to a religion of compassion, Scott allows for the bravery of the Scandinavian creed to play a role. It is, in this context, worth considering Andrew Lincoln's thoughts on Scott's novels, specifically his reluctance to reject 'unrefined passions' off-hand and instead use a historical perspective 'to allow a partial – and of course, heavily qualified – recovery of them', so that 'the vulgar' is re-established 'on manageable terms'.[12] We may discern in *Harold the Dauntless* a trajectory for a new Britain that incorporates Harold's heroism with Christian virtue to produce a heroic ideal for the modern age, not unlike what Edmund Burke identified as 'manly sentiment and heroic enterprize', which he saw as the touchstones for Europe.[13] For Scott, heroism in fiction was a feature of the Gothic tales. In connection with his historical novel *Waverley* (1814), which takes place only 60 years before the time of publication, Scott suggests that the idea for the novel originated in Horace Walpole's Gothic: 'I had nourished the ambitious desire of composing a tale of chivalry, which was to be in the style of the Castle of Otranto'.[14]

Like the hyperbolic and fanciful depictions of supernatural figures and events in Horace Walpole's foundational novel, Heather O'Donoghue has aptly observed that Scott's allusions to Norse myth have a 'comic book quality'.[15] The story of demonic spirits is relayed to us by a minstrel. Yet no one would have mistaken

---

11 Ibid., 194.
12 Andrew Lincoln, *Walter Scott and Modernity* (Edinburgh: Edinburgh University Press, 2007), 23.
13 Edmund Burke, *Reflections on the Revolution in France*, ed. L. G. Mitchell, vol. 8 in *The Writings and Speeches of Edmund Burke* (Oxford: Clarendon, 1989), 127.
14 Walter Scott, *Tales and Romances of the Author of Waverley* (Edinburgh: Robert Cadell, 1833), 8.
15 Heather O'Donoghue, *English Poetry and Old Norse Myth: A History* (Oxford: Oxford University Press, 2014), 126.

it for a translation of an ancient narrative. In fact, the framing of the poem underscores the ironic quality that permeates it, as the minstrel whimsically dismisses the unsolemn nature of his song in the opening lines. We may understand Scott's approach from a literary historical perspective. The text was published at a time, at the end of the second decade of the nineteenth century, when the Gothic was falling out of favour with the book-buying public. As Kerstin-Anja Münderlein notes, the decline simultaneously saw the rise of Gothic parody – as a reaction – until both Gothic and its parody were surpassed by other kinds of fiction writing.[16] It was with the historical novel that Scott made his name, of course – although Fiona Robertson shows that he incorporates Gothic tropes and scenes within his historical framework.[17] *Harold the Dauntless* is a poem in the tradition of the tall tale where the hero can battle with giants and other supernatural creatures. Yet it is precisely through this dismantling of historical accuracy that Scott can invite the reader to understand the narrative as a symbolic representation of the nation's history and the shifts it has undergone.

Traditions among Peripheral Communities

If Harold shows little regret when abandoning his pagan faith, Scott elsewhere imbues the depiction of Britain's pre-Christian legacy with a profound sense of painful nostalgia, showing how vestiges of Norse religion persisted in Scotland's periphery for generations after its formal replacement by the Christian church. His 1822 novel *The Pirate* is about the survival of Norse beliefs into the late seventeenth century and includes several Gothic moments of Norse terror. However, before we reach Scott's novel, it is useful to look at another representation of Scotland and how the memory of its Scandinavian settlers, especially in the archipelago of the Orkney and Shetland Islands off the north coast of mainland Scotland, continued to haunt and disturb the otherwise confident Christian nation. This is thematised in Agnes Musgrave's novel *Edmund of the Forest* (1797). Here, we encounter a trio of Shakespeare-inspired witches who warn the historical James III (King of Scots, 1460–88) about the plot against him led by his own son. The section of the novel featuring the witches contained sufficient Gothic dramatics to be excerpted for inclusion in the widely read collection *Gothic Stories* (1799).

---

16 Kerstin-Anja Münderlein, *Genre and Reception in the Gothic Parody: Framing the Subversive Heroine* (New York: Routledge, 2021), 58.

17 For a presentation of this argument, see Fiona Robertson, 'Gothic Scott', in *Scottish Gothic: An Edinburgh Companion*, ed. Carol Margaret Davison and Monica Germanà (Edinburgh: Edinburgh University Press, 2017), 102–14.

The section chosen for reprinting in this collection describes how Scotland still displayed the influence of 'the Danes, who possessed the Orcades'.[18] Even 'long after the light of christianity [*sic*] was spread over Scotland', the 'inmost gloomy recess' of the Scottish forest was rumoured to have 'the remains of a palace of those pagan kings, where still it is told dwell women who mock at our holy religion' and where 'barbarous and bloody rites were practised'.[19] The 'three hags' who inhabit this space are despised as supernatural remnants of a bygone era, rejected by a nation that has discarded such practices. Yet the past reaches into the present as embodied in the witches' contradictory appearance: they are 'deeply furrowed with wrinkles' while maintaining a gait that is 'strait and erect and betrayed no tokens of age'.[20] The depiction of witches occupying an atemporal domain symbolises the fact that the existence of the Scandinavians and their pagan ways is an unsettled historical legacy that refuses to be conclusively relegated to the past.

The fact that Norse paganism persisted as a minority religion in the northern parts of Scotland into relatively recent times fascinated Scott. In the summer of 1814, he embarked on a six-week trip that took him to Orkneys and the Hebrides with a company of the Commissioners of the Northern Lights (inspecting lighthouses). *The Pirate*, the novel that is the result of this journey, is set at the end of the seventeenth century, primarily in the Shetlands but also in the Orkneys. The novel was a runaway success with the audience (less so with the critics) and remained popular throughout the nineteenth century with numerous reprints. It is a love story centring around two half-brothers, Mordaunt and Cleveland, and their affection for Minna and Brenda, the daughters of Magnus Troil. The family of the Troils are the local rulers and descendants of the old Norse ruling class in the Northern Isles.

What is of interest here is the subtheme exploring the conflict between residual 'ancient northern superstition', i.e. the 'original veneration for those possessed of, or affecting supernatural knowledge', and a modern Scottish culture of Calvinism and mercantilism.[21] There is the bard, Claud Halcro, who cannot 'rid himself of his native superstitions' and sings in Norn (the now-extinct Norse language of Orkney, Shetland and parts of North Scotland) about the pixies, nixies and phantoms.[22]

---

18 'The adventure James III. of Scotland had with the weird sisters in the dreadful wood of Birnan', in *Gothic Stories* (London: S. Fisher, 1799), 16–22 (18).

19 Ibid.

20 Ibid., 20.

21 Walter Scott, *The Pirate*, ed. Mark Weinstein and Alison Lumsden (Edinburgh: Edinburgh University Press, 2001), 50.

22 Ibid., 224.

If Agnes Musgrave's novel had supernatural Norse witches roaming in the forests of Scotland, then Scott humanises this idea in Ulla Troil, known as Norna of the Fitful-head. She is a seeress of the old religion in the community, and a memory of a bygone era that lingers on in this peripheral region of Britain. Ulla is Scott's excuse to reference Norse supernaturalism – for example, her 'wild Runic rhyme', which resembles the verses sung by 'the heathen priests of old when the victim (too often human) was bound to the fatal altar of Odin or Thor'.[23] The many Scandinavian superstitions that flourished in the Northern Isles not long ago are detailed in Scott's antiquarian notes to the narrative. Despite the historical setting, there are several Gothic moments in the novel, such as when Ulla violates the tomb of her fifteenth-century ancestors to obtain a piece of metal from his coffin, commanding him not to wake from his slumber.[24] This scene riffs on the legend of Hervǫr intruding on dead father Angantyr's grave, which was discussed in Chapter 1.

However, Ulla discovers the limit of her imagined powers. She learns that she has failed to divine that Captain Cleveland (the 'pirate' of the novel), who has arrived on the island, is her lost son. She also discovers that she has unwittingly engineered his capture, which will lead to his execution. This realisation causes her to give up her role as a prophetess. Subsequently, she devotes herself to the study of the Bible, which was 'seldom laid aside'.[25] Scott employs the character of Ulla in his novel as a focal point for the fading collective memory of the Norse tradition on the verge of extinction in the late seventeenth century. Her character shows how a bridge between the old and the new is possible by integrating individual identities within a changing society. According to Robert Miles, Scott introduces an 'anti-Gothic' inclination in his novels, which is the historical understanding of development; it is 'a Burkean process in which the present emerges out of the past, as a continuous growth'.[26] This is what we see happen in *The Pirate*, as the old Scandinavian beliefs are shown as inefficient in dealing with present-day problems that one may encounter in modern Scotland.

Compared with *Harold the Dauntless*, Scott displays a more sensitive understanding of what is lost in *The Pirate*. In the castle of Seven Shields,

---

23 Ibid., 176.
24 Ibid., 240–41.
25 Ibid., 389.
26 Robert Miles, 'Gothic and Anti-Gothic, 1797–1820', in *The Oxford History of the Novel in English: Volume 2: English and British Fiction 1750–1820*, ed. Peter Garside and Karen O'Brien (Oxford: Oxford University Press, 2015), 234–54 (248).

the spirit of Odin tries to lure Harold back to the world of paganism he is set on abandoning with promises of warrior boons: 'Victory and vengeance', the 'joys' of Valhalla where immortal warriors can fight eternally and the pleasure of drinking the 'brimming draught from foeman's scull'.[27] Regarding Ulla abandoning the creed that provided her with an identity, readers are left with a different sense of wistfulness. As we see it across the Waverley novels, Scott shows sympathy with the demise of failing cultures, even if they are built on mistaken precepts, as they are always a painful loss for their adherents. At one point, Ulla is confronted by Mordaunt Merton, a representative of the modern Scottish gentry, who implores her to relinquish her adherence to Norse supernaturalism. In response, she articulates a poignant defence that unveils the profound motives behind a waning culture's tenacious embrace of archaic customs. She compares Mordaunt's invitation to abandon her faith to 'an insurrection in an invaded country' against the 'sovereignty' of someone who rules over 'gibbering ghosts, and howling winds, and raging currents'.[28] She concedes that 'my throne is a cloud, my sceptre a meteor, my realm is only peopled with fantasies', yet 'I must either cease to be, or continue to be the mightiest as well as the most miserable of beings! [...] I have no alternative, no middle station'.[29] Ulla's declaration is one of the most perceptive insights into a recurring theme in the Waverley series of losing cultures confronted with impending annihilation in the relentless progress of modernity. Scott reframes historical events partly from the perspective of a marginalised culture rather than solely adhering to dominant narratives of modernity. The novels recognise the agency and experience of the losers rather than casting them merely as obstructors of modernity.

Odin's Chosen One: Heroism on Salisbury Plain

The final text to be considered also includes the defeat of paganism's hold on Britain in a symbolic narrative about progress from darkness to light. It is the 66 stanza poem *Salisbury Plains*, with the subtitle *Stonehenge*, written by Ann Radcliffe, who was the most popular writer of Gothic novels. The poem was published posthumously in 1826.[30] It is an aetiological fantasy about

---

27 Scott, *Harold*, 192.
28 Ibid., 310.
29 Ibid., 310–11.
30 Ann Radcliffe, *Gaston de Blondeville: or The Court of Henry III . . . with Some Poetical Pieces*, vol. 4 (London: H. Colburn, 1826), 109–61. Henceforth, page references to this work will be given in brackets within the text.

the origin of Stonehenge. Radcliffe crafts a tale set in ancient times, including the involvement of the god Odin. However, unlike in Scott's poem, where Odin is depicted as a figure that Harold battles against, he is portrayed as primarily a positive force. I argue that the religion of Odin is here inserted for its association with a commitment to liberty, which becomes a first step in the history of Britain's progress. Although Odin plays a positive role, the power of Christianity will eventually triumph over paganism.

The story takes place on Salisbury Plain, which is cursed by evil forces. The geographical area in question covers approximately 300 square miles in south-western England, and its barrenness also inspired William Wordsworth's dark poem 'Guilt and Sorrow; or, Incidents upon Salisbury Plain' (1842) with its images of sacrifices at Stonehenge to forgotten pagan gods. Radcliffe's poem takes us back to a mythical time when the plain was reigned by supernatural beings. Warwolf is a powerful dragon-like sorcerer who draws strength from Hela, the queen of the Norse underworld, and the malevolent god Loki. The poem narrates the story of an unnamed hermit living on Salisbury Plain. Odin, the leader of Germanic gods, chooses the hermit to defeat Warwolf and break his tyrannical hold over the land. The hermit journeys courageously to Warwolf's lair to extract his 140 teeth, wherein his power resides. This becomes the Gothic climax of Radcliffe's poem, as the intense and dangerous removal of teeth in the dark lair of the Wizard is described in vivid detail. The hermit manages this task before the Wizard wakes and can finally bury the fangs nine fathoms deep on Salisbury Plain. However, Warwolf's dark spells have turned the plain into a barren land, and his fangs have magically grown in size to form the formation now known as Stonehenge. The protection against evil lasts as long as the Druid race is alive, but when they die out, '[f]iendish sprites' begin to 'ride on the air', and the harvests are cursed (153). At the poem's end, the local people build Salisbury Cathedral, whose spires will 'watch and wake' (157) and guard the land for posterity.

Edmund Burke mentioned Stonehenge as an example of the sublime.[31] In Radcliffe's poem, the sublime also plays a significant role. When the hermit wanders the plain and first realises that the teeth have magically grown, he is awestruck by their anthropomorphic appearance: 'What dark and mighty shapes are those, / Standing like dæmons of the night? [...] A lofty and motionless giant-band!' (148). From the hermit's first reaction, the poem moves to the monument's importance as a sublime

---

31 Edmund Burke, *A Philosophical Enquiry into the Origin of Our Ideas of the Sublime and Beautiful* (London: R. and J. Dodsley, 1757), 60.

construction in the national consciousness: 'High wonder filled his mind, as this he saw / And wonder still and reverential awe, / From age to age, have filled the gazer's mind' (148).

The contrast Radcliffe holds up to it is Salisbury Cathedral (which was famously the subject of a painting by John Constable in 1823). The Christian building surpasses the pagan monument in sublimity with its 'form so majestic so gracefully fine' and spire 'viewed by the dawn's blue light / Or rising darkly on the night / As with tall black line to measure the sphere' (155). Thereby, as soon as bands of demons spy the 'watching eye' of the cathedral, 'Sullen they sigh and shrink and fly' (157). Thus, through her storytelling, Radcliffe creates a mythopoetic narrative about the iconic structure of Stonehenge, imbuing it with symbolic resonance as a testament to the struggle for liberty. The poem reinforces the national narrative that Britain defanged dark forces armed with the Gothic race's inherent ideals of liberty, ultimately accepting the rule of Christianity as the final triumph over darkness.

It is plausible that the poem shows Radcliffe's interest in representing the legacy of Odin in England in accordance with how he becomes a symbol of liberty in Paul-Henri Mallet's *Northern Antiquities* – a work Radcliffe quotes in the notes to the poem. Warwolf is cast as a 'tyrant-dæmon' (151), while Odin is the compassionate leader who 'has heard his people's groan' (120) under Warwolf's reign. Odin's aiding the Druid to end Warwolf's occupation of Salisbury Plain is in line with Mallet's representation of Odin as a human warlord who inspired Northern rebels to overthrow the Roman Empire, the 'enemies of universal liberty'.[32] And through the worship of Odin, 'a plan of liberty' became 'the peculiar honour of all the Gothic tribes'.[33] This idea was celebrated by British writers at the time, such as in Robert Southey's poem 'The Race of Odin', which celebrates the 'Freedom' that 'beheld the noble race' of Odin's people and 'fill'd each bosom with her vivid fire'.[34] For them, 'Danger could ne'er the nation daunt', and they are therefore set upon defeating imperial Rome in a symbolic victory after which 'the world again is free!'.[35] Radcliffe similarly invokes Odin as a metaphor for the struggle against oppressive forces that once held the land. We may ask if

32 Paul-Henri Mallet, *Northern Antiquities: or, A Description of the Manners, Customs, Religion and Laws of the Ancient Danes, and Other Northern Nations; Including Those of Our Own Saxon Ancestors* (London: T. Carnan, 1770), 1:67.

33 Thomas Percy's preface in ibid, 1:xii–xiii.

34 Robert Southey and Robert Lovel, *Poems: Containing The Retrospect, Odes, Elegies, Sonnets, &c.* (London: C. Dilly, 1795), 99.

35 Ibid., 102.

Warwolf is Radcliffe's allegory of the occupying Romans (the Roman image of the Capitoline Wolf transmogrified into a monster?). In any case, the final lesson is that liberty also requires freeing the mind from superstition through Christianity. Thus, the final taming of Stonehenge's dark power must be the Church.

In creating a tale of ancient, mythical Britain, Radcliffe wanted to underscore liberty as a value originating from and persisting innately within the collective racial soul in ways that align with J. G. Herder's formative ideas on national psychology. The ideal of liberty could thus point forward to the libertarian traditions so central to British constitutionalism. For this reason, Odin is imagined as a god native to Britain rather than an exogenous influence transplanted to Britain with the Viking invaders. To make this narrative work, Radcliffe undertakes a rather difficult historical revision. The dominant opinion of Radcliffe's day followed John Aubrey's interpretation in *Monumenta Britannica* (1663–93), which was that Druids built Stonehenge.[36] Therefore, we learn that the hermit, who heeds Odin's call to free the land, was believed to be 'the first of all the Druid race' (118). This is historically erroneous, as Druids were a priesthood in the Celto-Brittonic tradition. Evidently, Radcliffe shows her awareness of this problem in the line: 'Some stories say a Druid never bent / At Odin's shrine' (118). Radcliffe can be understood to construct a vision of indigenous ideals that formed an ancient and indestructible bedrock beneath Britain's growth into a guardian of constitutional liberty.

Radcliffe attempts to turn the mystical, physical edifice into what the French historian Pierre Nora calls a *lieu de mémoire*, a site of memory that is an element of memorial heritage for the nation. Radcliffe notes that we know Stonehenge to be the name of the structure on Salisbury Plain, but 'what more it means no man may say' (148). To use Paul Connerton's terminology, the monumental presence of Stonehenge was 'incorporated' (experienced and sensed through the body) in the national psyche but lacked an encapsulating story (a narrative adding a mnemonic value to the site).[37] Radcliffe's story is crafted to provide precisely a story about the sublime, mysterious structure in a Gothic register. Like the looming edifices of old castles that came to be metaphors for the hierarchies and restrictive customs of feudalism and patriarchal rule, Stonehenge

---

36 Kelsey Jackson Williams, *The Antiquary: John Aubrey's Historical Scholarship* (Oxford: Oxford University Press, 2016), 20–45.

37 Paul Connerton, *How Modernity Forgets* (Cambridge: Cambridge University Press, 2009), esp. 13 and 33.

becomes a monument symbolising the defeat of tyrannical governance and oppression. As in the other example in this chapter, Radcliffe picks a scene from British history that can be seen emblematically to contribute to understanding the modern nation.

Conclusion

The writers of the Gothic texts examined above deployed the pagan tradition that was part of Britain's history as a shadowy 'Other' associated with the supernatural, violence and the irrational. While the texts mark paganism's abandonment and celebrate the triumph of Christianity, they also indicate that ghosts of the Danes and their influence have been insufficiently acknowledged in Britain's telling of its own history. For Wordsworth, for instance, the melancholic singing of the Danish boy can be read as an acknowledgement of the lingering cultural memory of Danish settlement in the Lake District, a distinct characteristic of this regional landscape. Regional uniqueness is a question of grappling with the heritage of the pagan past, as is the case when Scott sets the scene of *Harold the Dauntless* in Durham, or Radcliffe, with her childhood connections to Bath, focuses on the West Country.

The literary accounts of the Scandinavian invaders are multifaceted rather than simply negative. There is the sense that the literary tales can address what official records have largely failed to recognise: Danes may initially have been invaders, but their settlement contributed to creating a melting pot of peoples who collectively engaged in forging new permutations and possibly productive reshaping of culture. Scott's *Harold the Dauntless* focuses on a character who converts to new Christian values, exemplifying the transformative power that the nation is believed to possess in its progress towards modernity. Both Scott and Radcliffe highlight the virtues of heroism and liberty, for which the Nordic people's Odinic religion was recognised. These are values that British writers would generally co-opt for British history; it becomes a legacy that lingers whilst the paganism is discarded.

We see that the pagan Danes in some of the texts are used as symbols that foreshadow the evolution of modern Britain as a melting pot of diverse nationalities unified through the communal embrace of shared religious values. If the wilder superstitions of the pagan Danes were overcome – as ever must be through civilising progress – one ought not to forget that those unruly beliefs also fed an indomitable spirit that infused ancestors with courage and a love of liberty from which (it is indicated) the nation may beget its resilience and strength of character. In all the texts, there is a recognition that modern Britain has been shaped as the result of a conflicted past, but if such conflict is inevitable, it may produce, dialectically, a higher unity. The texts are each attuned to subterranean currents of the Gothic mode and can express (through symbolic scenes and allegorical narratives) a flavour of Norse religion missing from factual chronicling. The texts address a different and more nuanced aspect of Danish or pagan culture in Britain, positioning it meaningfully within a larger historical vector of progress.

POSTSCRIPT

The history of how the terrors of Scandinavia became a recognisable reference in British literary Gothic production has lacked focused attention from critics. Therefore, the purpose of the present book has been to analyse how mythology and superstition from Nordic/Scandinavian sources were utilised to provide a new archive of terror. That much of the material was sourced from or inspired by authentic texts raises important questions about how cultural appropriation and dialogue with the past shape literary traditions, and how ideas, themes and motifs travel across borders and time periods to shape the artistic and intellectual landscape in late eighteenth- and early nineteenth centuries. I offer my findings as a contribution to the understanding of cultural and literary reinvigoration in the period.

Before the emergence of Gothic literature as a fashionable mode of writing, the idea of Britain as part of an ethno-Gothic cultural zone already played a significant role in history writing. The Norse tradition held the most comprehensive archive of pre-Christian beliefs associated with this tradition, followed by the remnants of superstition and the fairy ways recorded in folk ballads. This notion of cultural legacy was reinforced by the fact that the British Isles had been comprehensively settled by Scandinavians – the meaning of which was in the process of being reinterpreted for British culture. It has been a key argument throughout that what became recognised as 'Scandinavian' terror was more than just substituting one abject 'Other' for another. While British writers could gloat at the wayward phantasms and delusions, as they could with, for example, Catholic excesses, Scandinavian texts and practices were accepted as a window to the pre-Christian beliefs of the Gothic/Germanic ancestors, which included the Anglo-Saxons. As a cultural response to the Celtic Ossian poems, ancient Scandinavian poetry was seen not primarily as a flirtation with foreign ideas but as a recovery of a native voice.

I have proposed that an important catalyst for promoting Norse terror was the response it was believed to provide to the more sentimental Ossian literature, which became a sensation in the 1760s. Norse terror was an intervention favouring what was promoted as a daring and masculine ethno-Gothic heritage. The fearless attitude of the ancestors in confronting danger, not least the otherworldly kind, became a prominent theme in how the tradition was received, and it determined what was selected for translation. Whether the Norse ancestors faced the terrors of the undead or encountered supernatural beings, the Norse warriors' unwavering courage served as an example of their bravery and unwavering spirit. Alongside the interest in promoting the Gothic (and thereby the Anglo-Saxon) past, a complementary impulse was to establish a venerable lineage for English literature, as Norse imagination was seen as representing the thought and manners of pre-Christian Britain. The past could also serve the present. There was a gradual realisation, which became manifest in the last decades of the eighteenth century, that Britain's rich imaginative inheritance could be mined and reclaimed in an attempt to break free from the rigid conventions of neoclassicism.

By delving into Nordic legends as proxies for Britain's own archaeology of myth and folklore, one may tap symbolic springs from where modern humans' psychologies derive. Therein, deep-rooted terrors could be traded, traditions reinvigorated and audiences intrigued through confrontation with a version of their own forgotten selves. However, the relationship between the culturally motivated interest in the ancestral past and the opportunities created by the book market for terror is multifaceted. This study has shown that the boundary between historical interest and mercantile exploitation is not always clear-cut.

In particular, folklore ballads became fashionable literary items. Matthew Lewis enhanced the fragments of Danish balladry he could get hold of (through German translation) by establishing a supernatural cosmology of elemental 'kings', which had no origin in the original material. Ballads that contained magic or supernatural elements, what Nathan Drake calls the 'vulgar Gothic', represented a tradition associated with the lower orders, harbouring a residue of irrationality that threatened to unsettle Britain's hallowed sense of modernity. Thus, as part of the inventive reassembling of Danish folklore, Lewis incorporated satire to mitigate cultural anxieties. The reception of Scandinavian traditions always navigated the uneasy road between appealing to a historical desire to recapture autochthonous cultural roots and a drive to set British rationalities apart from its superstitious past. This problem area is worked out in various ways in relation to one of the most frequently translated ballads drawing on folklore material, J. W. Goethe's 'Erlkönig' (1782). This is an imitation inspired by J. G. Herder's translation of a Danish ballad but reimagined so that it now questions whether ballad supernaturalism is real or exists only in the imagination of the superstitious individual. The figure (or figment) of the malignant forest fiend in Goethe's ballad was adapted to become a menacing character in Lewis' melodrama *One O'Clock! Or, The Knight and the Wood-Daemon* (1811). If this play relied on folklore terror for its plot, the narrative ultimately conveys modernity's triumph over a ritualistic and irrational past. In this context, we may discern a difference in how Norse tradition and Scandinavian folklore were represented. While Norse texts projected a sense of nobility by depicting ancient heroes undaunted in facing sublime terrors – an ethnocultural trait that could be celebrated – the folklore ballad exemplified a more recent superstition still present in some layers of society. Thus, it was treated with more suspicion, and the ballads became something to be observed from a distance, calling for defensive cautiousness.

Although enemies of superstition, Walter Scott and Ann Radcliffe both attempted to find a place for the Scandinavian past in British history beyond irrationalism. In narrative poems and novels, we see recognition of the Scandinavians who once peopled the British Isles and their reputed dedication to freedom as forming part of a national legacy. Nonetheless, the nation's transformative progress towards enlightened Christianity is a source of national strength and unity is emphasised above all else. However, Norse beliefs were linked to a resolute spirit that was welcomed when freed from their superstitious associations. Going back in time to fictional historical events when superstition was defeated is also to uncover old reservoirs of resilience and courage that were believed to sustain Britain's unique historical genius.

This study has documented how ethno-Gothic beliefs provided texts with material for literary Gothic writing. However, using Norse or Scandinavian traditions in the guise of terror literature signified a complex cultural moment in Britain. The nuanced examination I hope to have demonstrated in this book shows that the use of ancestral terrors was dependent on contexts. Ultimately, the appeal that the Nordic past had to the age was anchored less to a singular cultural ideology than to where revivalists strategically placed it among the period's prevailing discourses.

BIBLIOGRAPHY

Addison, Joseph. *The Spectator*, no. 419 (1 July 1712), vol. 6, 127. London: S. Buckley and J. Tonson, 1713.

'The adventure James III. of Scotland had with the weird sisters in the dreadful wood of Birnan'. In *Gothic Stories*. 16–22. London: S. Fisher, 1799.

Arnold, Martin. 'On the Origins of the Gothic Novel: From Old Norse to Otranto'. In *Bram Stoker and the Gothic: Formations to Transformations*, edited by Catherine Wynne, 14–29. Houndsmills: Palgrave, 2016.

Backscheider, Paula. *Spectacular Politics: Theatrical Power and Mass Culture in Early Modern England*, Baltimore: Johns Hopkins University Press, 1993.

Baldick, Chris and Robert Mighall, 'Gothic Criticism'. In *The New Companion to the Gothic*, edited by David Punter, 267–87. Hoboken, NJ: Wiley-Blackwell, 2012.

Bannerman, Anne. *Tales of Superstition and Chivalry*. London: Vernor and Hood, 1802.

Bartholin, Thomas. *Antiqvitatum Danicarum de causis contempta a Danis adhuc gentilibus mortis*. Hafnia: J. Phil. Bockenhoffer, 1689.

Beckford, William. *An Arabian Tale: From an unpublished manuscript with notes critical and explanatory*. London: J. Johnson, 1786.

Bezrucka, Yvonne. *The Invention of Northern Aesthetics in 18th-Century English Literature*. Newcastle upon Tyne: Cambridge Scholars Publishing, 2017.

Boyd, Henry. 'The Witch of Lapland', *The Annual Register* 56 (1806): 905–7.

Brand, John and Henry Bourne. *Observations on Popular Antiquities*. London: J. Johnson, 1777.

Bridgewater, Patrick. *The German Gothic Novel in Anglo-German Perspective*. Amsterdam: Rodopi, 2013.

Burke, Edmund. *A Philosophical Enquiry into the Origin of Our Ideas of the Sublime and Beautiful*. London: R. and J. Dodsley, 1757.

——— 'Reflections on the Revolution in France', In *The Writings and Speeches of Edmund Burke*, vol. 8, edited by L. G. Mitchell. Oxford: Clarendon, 1989.

Burnett, Linda Andersson. 'Selling the Sami: Nordic Stereotypes and Participatory Media in Georgian Britain'. In *Communicating the North: Media Structures and Images in the Making of the Northern Region*, edited by Jonas Harvard and Peter Stadius, 171–96. Farnham: Ashgate, 2013.

Burwick, Frederick. *Time in Romantic Theatre*. Cham: Palgrave, 2022.

Collins, William. 'An Ode on the Popular Superstitions of the Highlands of Scotland, Considered as the Subject of Poetry', edited by Alexander Carlyle. In *Transactions of the Royal Society of Edinburgh*, vol. 1, 63–75. Edinburgh: J. Dickson, 1788.

Cottle, Joseph. *Alfred, an Epic Poem, in Twenty-Four Books*, 2nd ed. London: Longman and Rees, 1800.

Cox, Jeffrey M. 'Gothic Drama: Tragedy or Comedy'. In *The Oxford Handbook of the Georgian Theatre 1737–1832*, edited by Julia Swindells and David Francis Taylor, 407–23. Oxford: Oxford University Press, 2014.

Craig, Steven. 'Shakespeare among the Goths'. In *Gothic Shakespeares*, edited by John Drakakis and Dale Townshend, 42–59. Abingdon: Routledge, 2008.

Curley, Thomas M. *Samuel Johnson, the Ossian Fraud, and the Celtic Revival in Great Britain and Ireland*. Cambridge: Cambridge University Press, 2009.

Cusack, Andrew and Barry Murnane, Eds. *Popular Revenants: The German Gothic and Its International Reception, 1800–2000*. Rochester: Camden House, 2012.

Daniel, Carolyn. *Voracious Children: Who Eats Whom in Children's Literature*. New York: Routledge, 2006.

Davison, Carol Margaret. 'The Politics and Poetics of the "Scottish Gothic" from Ossian to Otranto and Beyond'. In *Scottish Gothic: An Edinburgh Companion*, edited by Carol Margaret Davison and Monica Germanà, 28–41. Edinburgh: Edinburgh University Press, 2017.

Dibdin, Thomas John. 'Harlequin's Magnet; or, Scandinavian Sorcerer', manuscript in the Huntington Library, https://www.eighteenthcenturydrama.amdigital.co.uk/Documents/Details/HL_LA_mssLA1468.

Drakakis, John and Dale Townshend, Eds. *Gothic Shakespeares*. Abingdon: Routledge, 2008.

Drake, Nathan. *Literary Hours: Or, Sketches Critical and Narrative*. London: T. Cadell, 1798.

Edmund and Velina, a Legendary Tale. And Albert and Ellen, a Danish Ballad. Edinburgh: Archibald Constable, 1797.

'Eulogium of Hacon, King of Norway', *The Massachusetts Magazine* (September 1791): 564–65.

Farley, F. E. Scandinavian Influences in the English Romantic Movement. Boston, MA: Ginn & Co., 1903.

Favret, Mary A. *War at a Distance: Romanticism and the Making of Modern Wartime*. Princeton, NJ: Princeton University Press, 2009.

Gamer, Michael. *Romanticism and the Gothic: Genre, Reception, and Canon Formation*. Cambridge: Cambridge University Press, 2000.

——— 'Gothic Melodrama'. In *The Cambridge Companion to English Melodrama*, edited by Carolyn Williams, 31–46. Cambridge: Cambridge University Press, 2018.

Glover, Gareth. *The Two Battles of Copenhagen, 1801 And 1807: Britain and Denmark in the Napoleonic Wars*. Barnsley: Pen & Sword Books, 2018.

Grant, Anne. *Essays on the Superstitions of the Highlanders of Scotland*, 2 vols. London: Longman et al. 1811.

Gray, Thomas. *Poems by Mr. Gray, A New Edition*. London: J. Dodsley, 1768.

——— *The Poems of Thomas Gray. To Which are Prefixed Memoirs of His Life and Writings by W. Mason*, 2 vols. Dublin: D. Chamberlaine et. al., 1775.

——— *The Works of Thomas Gray: The Poems with Critical Notes*. London: J. Mawman, 1816.

——— Commonplace Book, vol. 3, p. 56v, Cambridge University Digital Library, https://cudl.lib.cam.ac.uk/view/MS-PEMBROKE-GRA-00001-00003/1.

Grimm, Jacob. *Teutonic Mythology*, trans. James Steven Stallybrass, 4 vols. London: George Bell and Sons, 1883.

Hansford, Roger. *Figures of the Imagination: Fiction and Song in Britain, 1790–1850*. London: Routledge, 2017.

Harris, Jason Marc. *Folklore and the Fantastic in Nineteenth-Century British Fiction*. London: Routledge, 2016.

Hart, Carina. 'Gothic Folklore and Fairy Tale: Negative Nostalgia', *Gothic Studies* 22, no. 1 (2020): 1–13.

Hartman, Geoffrey. 'Wordsworth and Goethe in Literary History', *New Literary History* 6, no. 2 (1975): 393–413.

Hayley, William. *An Essay on Epic Poetry, in Five Epistles*. Dublin: S. Price et al., 1782.

Heine, Heinrich, *The Works of Heinrich Heine*, vol. 6, translated by Charles Godfrey Leland. London: William Heinemann, 1892.

Henry, Robert. *The History of Great Britain*, vol. 3. London: T. Cadell, and W. Davies, 1805.

Herder, Johann Gottfried. *Volkslieder*, 2 vols. Leipzig: Weygand, 1778.

——— 'Iduna, oder der Apfel der Verjüngung', *Die Horen: Eine Monatsschrift* 5 (1796): 1–28.

Hilliard, Raymond F. *Ritual Violence and the Maternal in the British Novel, 1740–1820*. Lewisburg, PA.: Bucknell University Press, 2010.

Hoeveler, Diane Long. 'The Temple of Morality: Thomas Holcroft and the Swerve of Melodrama', *European Romantic Review* 14, no. 1 (2003): 49–63.

——— *Gothic Riffs: Secularizing the Uncanny in the European Imaginary, 1780–1820*. Columbus, OH: Ohio State University Press, 2010.

Hole, Richard. 'The Tomb of Gunnar. Imitated from an Ancient Islandic Fragment, preserved by Bartholin', *Gentleman's Magazine* (October 1789): 937.

——— *Arthur, or, The Northern Enchantments*. London: G. G. J. and J. Robinson, 1789.

Hurd, Richard. *Letters on Chivalry and Romance*. London: A. Millar, W. Thurlbourn, and J. Woodyer, 1762.

——— *Moral and Political Dialogues; with Letters on Chivalry and Romance*, 5th edition, volume 3. London: T. Cadell, 1776.

Jamieson, Robert. *Popular Ballads and Songs: From Tradition, Manuscripts and Scarce Editions; with Translations of Similar Pieces from the Ancient Danish Language, and a Few Originals by the Editor*, 2 vols. Edinburgh: A. Constable and Company, 1806.

Johnson, Samuel. 'Preface to *The Plays of William Shakespeare*' (1765). In *Selected Works*, edited by Robert DeMaria, Jr., Stephen Fix, and Howard D. Weinbrot, 425–62. New Haven: Yale University Press, 2021.

Kassis, Dimitrios. *Representations of the North in Victorian Travel Literature*. Newcastle upon Tyne, Cambridge Scholars, 2015.

Kidd, Colin. *Subverting Scotland's Past: Scottish Whig Historians and the Creation of an Anglo-British Identity 1689–1830*. Cambridge: Cambridge University Press, 1993.

——— *British Identities before Nationalism: Ethnicity and Nationhood in the Atlantic World, 1600–1800*. Cambridge: Cambridge University Press, 1999.

Lawrence, Rose. *The Last Autumn at a Favourite Residence: With Other Poems*. London: G. and J. Robinson; and Longman, Rees, Orme, Brown & Green, 1829.

Leffler, Yvonne. *Swedish Gothic: Landscapes of Untamed Nature*. London: Anthem Press, 2022.

Legends of Terror!: And Tales of the Wonderful and Wild. London: Sherwood, Gilbert, and Piper, 1826.

'Letter to the Editor: Vindication of the War against Denmark', *Flower's Political Review and Monthly Register* (November 1807): 314–17.

Lewis, Matthew Gregory. *The Monk: A Romance*, 3 vols. London: J. Bell, 1796.

——— 'The Erl-King', *The Monthly Mirror* 2 (October 1796): 371–73.

——— *Ambrosio, or the Monk: A Romance*, 3 vols. London: J. Bell, 1798.

——— *The Castle Spectre: A Drama*. London: J. Bell, 1798.

——— Ed. *Tales of Wonder*, 2 vols. London: J. Bell, 1801.

——— *Romantic Tales*, 3 vols. London: Longman, Hurst, Rees, and Orme, 1808.

────── *One O'Clock!, Or, the Knight and the Wood Dæmon. A Grand Musical Romance*. London: Lowndes and Hobbs, 1811.

Lincoln, Andrew. *Walter Scott and Modernity*. Edinburgh: Edinburgh University Press, 2007.

Lines, Sydney. 'Norse Romanticism: Subversive Female Voices in British Invocations of Nordic Yore', PhD thesis, Arizona State University, 2013.

Lovecraft, Howard Phillips. *Supernatural Horror in Literature*. Abergele: Wermod and Wermod Publishing Group, 2013.

Mackenzie, Anna Maria *Mysteries Elucidated. A Novel*, 3 vols. London: Minerva Press, 1795.

Macdonald, David Lorne *Monk Lewis: A Critical Biography*. Toronto: University of Toronto Press, 2000.

Mallet, Paul-Henri. *Northern Antiquities: Or, a Description of the Manners, Customs, Religion and Laws of the Ancient Danes, and Other Northern Nations; Including Those of Our Own Saxon Ancestors*, translated by Thomas Percy, 2 vols. London: T. Carnan and Co., 1770.

Mathias, Thomas James. *Runic Odes: Imitated from the Norse Tongue in the Manner of Mr. Gray*. London: T. Payne et al. 1781.

────── *Runic Odes from the Norse Tongue*. London: T. Becket, 1790.

────── *The Pursuits of Literature*, vol. 4. London: T. Becket, 1797.

────── *The Pursuits of Literature: A Satirical Poem in Four Dialogues*, 7th edn. London: T. Beckett, 1798.

Maturin, Charles. *Melmoth the Wanderer*. Oxford: Oxford University Press, 1998.

McCorristine, Shane. *Spectres of the Self: Thinking About Ghosts and Ghost-Seeing in England, 1750–1920*. Cambridge: Cambridge University Press, 2010.

Mazzeo, Tilar J. *Plagiarism and Literary Property in the Romantic Period*. Philadelphia, PA: University of Philadelphia Press, 2007.

Mehtonen, Paivi and Matti Savolainen, Eds. *Gothic Topographies: Language, Nation-Building and 'Race'*. Farnham: Ashgate, 2016.

Miles, Robert. 'Political Gothic Fiction'. In *Romantic Gothic: An Edinburgh Companion*, edited by Angela Wright and Dale Townshend, 129–46. Edinburgh: Edinburgh University Press, 2015.

────── 'Gothic and Anti-Gothic, 1797–1820'. In *The Oxford History of the Novel in English: Volume 2: English and British Fiction 1750–1820*, edited by Peter Garside and Karen O'Brien, 234–54. Oxford: Oxford University Press, 2015.

Møller, Lis. '"They dance all under the greenwood tree": British and Danish Romantic-Period Adaptations of Two Danish "Elf Ballads"'. In *Romantic Norths: Anglo-Nordic Exchanges, 1770–1842*, edited by Cian Duffy, 129–52. Cham: Palgrave, 2017.

────── 'Travelling Ballads: The Dissemination of Danish Medieval Ballads in Germany and Britain, 1760s to 1830s'. In *Danish Literature as World Literature*, edited by Dan Ringgaard and Mads Rosendahl Thomsen, 31–51. London: Bloomsbury Academic, 2017.

'Monody on the Death of Sir John Moore'. In *The Life and Correspondence of M.G. Lewis*, vol. 1, edited by Margaret Baron-Wilson, 380. London: Henry Colburn, 1839.

Moore, Dafydd. 'Patriotism, Politeness, and National Identity in the South West of England in the Late Eighteenth Century', *ELH* 76, no. 3 (2009): 739–62.

Mortensen, Peter. *British Romanticism and Continental Influences: Writing in an Age of Europhobia*. Basingstoke: Palgrave Macmillan, 2004.

Mumford, Lewis. *Technics and Civilization*. Chicago. Il: University of Chicago Press, 2010.

Münderlein, Kerstin-Anja. *Genre and Reception in the Gothic Parody: Framing the Subversive Heroine*. New York: Routledge, 2021.

Naubert, Benedikte. 'The Erl-King's Daughter'. In *Popular Tales and Romances of the Northern Nations*, vol. 3, 251–349. London: W. Simpkin et al. and R. Marshall.

Nicholls, Mark. '*Tales of Terror*, 1801'. In *Notes and Queries* NS 48, no. 2 (2001): 119–21.

Nordius, Janina. 'Introduction'. In Swedish *Mysteries, or, Hero of the Mines*, vii–xxx. Kansas City: Valancourt Books, 2008.

O'Donoghue, Heather. *English Poetry and Old Norse Myth: A History*. Oxford: Oxford University Press, 2014.

Omberg, Margaret. *Scandinavian Themes in English Poetry, 1760–1800*. Uppsala: Uppsala University, 1976.

One O'Clock; or, the Knight and the Wood Demon. Founded on the popular piece, of that name, as performed at the Theatres' Royal. London: G. Drake, c. 1840.

Parisot, Eric. 'The Aesthetics of Terror and Horror: A Genealogy'. In *The Cambridge History of the Gothic. Vol. 1: Gothic in the Long Eighteenth Century*, edited by Angela Wright and Dale Townshend, 284–303. Cambridge: Cambridge University Press, 2020.

Pearson, Rachael. 'Politics and Power in the Gothic Drama of M. G. Lewis', PhD thesis, University of Southampton, 2011.

Percy, Thomas, Ed. and Trans. *Five Pieces of Runic Poetry Translated from the Islandic Language*. London: R. Dodsley, 1763.

Pinkerton, John. *An Enquiry into the History of Scotland: Preceding the Reign of Malcolm III*, new ed. Edinburgh: Bell et al. 1814.

Polwhele, Richard. *Poems Chiefly by Gentlemen of Devonshire and Cornwall*, 2 vols. Bath: T. Cadell, 1792.

Porter, Anna Maria. 'The Erl; or, Oak King: A Danish Ballad', *The Monthly Visitor, and Entertaining Pocket Companion* (December 1797): 52–57.

Potter, Franz J. *The History of Gothic Publishing, 1800–1835: Exhuming the Trade*. Houndsmills: Palgrave, 2005.

Prior, R. C. Alexander. 'Introduction', In *Ancient Danish Ballads*, vol. 1, i–liv. London: Williams and Norgate, 1860.

Punter, David. *The Literature of Terror: History of Gothic Fiction from 1765 to the Present Day*. London: Longman, 1980.

Quinn, Judy and Maria Adele Cipolla, Eds. Studies in the Transmission and Reception of Old Norse Literature: The Hyperborean Muse in European Culture. Brepols: Turnhout, 2016.

Radcliffe, Ann. *Gaston de Blondeville: Or The Court of Henry III … with Some Poetical Pieces*, 4 vols. London: H. Colburn, 1826.

Ravenwood, Victoria. 'Historical anecdotes are the most proper vehicles for the elucidation of knowledge': The 'Historical Gothic' and the Minerva Press, 1790–99', *Romantic Textualities: Literature and Print Culture* 23 (2020): 1780–1840. https://www.romtext.org.uk/.

Ringgaard, Dan and Mads Rosendahl Thomsen, Eds., *Danish Literature as World Literature*. London: Bloomsbury, 2017.

Rix, Robert W. 'Oriental Odin: Tracing the East in Northern Culture and Literature', *History of European Ideas* 36, no. 1 (2010): 47–60.

——— 'Gothic Gothicism: Norse Terror in the Late Eighteenth to Early Nineteenth Centuries'. *Gothic Studies* 13, no. 1 (2011): 1–20.

———— 'The European Circulation of Nordic Texts in the Romantic Period', *Oxford Research Encyclopedias: Literature* (2017), 1–30. https://doi.org/10.1093/acrefore/9780190201098.013.294.

———— 'The Elf-King: Translation, Transmission, and Transfiguration'. In *Nordic Romanticism: Translation, Transmission, Transformation,* edited by Cian Duffy and Robert W. Rix, 1–30. Cham: Palgrave, 2022.

Robertson, Fiona. 'Gothic Scott' In *Scottish Gothic: An Edinburgh Companion,* edited by Carol Margaret Davison and Monica Germanà, 102–14. Edinburgh: Edinburgh University Press, 2017.

Roper, Jonathan. 'England – The Land without Folklore?'. In *Folklore and Nationalism in Europe During the Long Nineteenth Century,* edited by Timothy Baycroft and David Hopkin, 227–54. Boston: BRILL, 2012.

Ross, Margaret Clunies. *The Norse Muse in Britain: 1750–1820.* Parnaso: Trieste, 1998.

'The Rovers'. In *The Beauties of the Anti-Jacobin: Or, Weekly Examiner,* 251–79. London: C. Chapple, 1799.

Rutherford, Brett. 'Introduction to Volume II'. In *Tales of Wonder,* vol. 2, 2nd ed., edited by Matthew Lewis, xii–xvi. Pittsburgh, PA: Poet's Press, 2017.

Sayers, Frank. *Dramatic Sketches of the Ancient Northern Mythology.* London: Joseph Johnson, 1790.

Schmitt, Cannon. *Alien Nation: Nineteenth-Century Gothic Fictions and English Nationality.* Philadelphia, PA: University of Pennsylvania Press, 1997.

Schneider, Christian Frederik, *Danish Grammar Adapted to the Use of Englishmen.* Copenhagen: F. Brummer, 1799.

Scott, Walter. *Apology for Tales of Terror.* Kelso: Printed at the Mail Office, 1799.

———— 'Review of *Report of the Highland Society of Scotland … and the Poems of Ossian … Works of James Macpherson*'. *Edinburgh Review* 6, no. 12 (July 1805): 429–62.

———— *The Lay of the Last Minstrel: A Poem,* 3rd ed. London: Longman et al., 1806.

———— 'Introduction to the Tale of Tamlane. On the Fairies of Popular Superstition'. In *Minstrelsy of the Scottish Border,* vol. 2, 109–86. Edinburgh: James Ballantyne, 1810.

———— *The Lady of the Lake: A Poem.* Edinburgh: John Ballantyne, 1810.

———— *Harold the Dauntless. A Poem in Six Cantos.* London: Longman, Hurst, Rees, Orme and Brown, 1817.

———— 'Imitations of the Ancient Ballads'. In *Minstrelsy of the Scottish Border,* 5 ed., vol. 1, 3–83. London: Longman et al., 1821.

———— *Letters on Demonology and Witchcraft.* London: John Murray, 1830.

———— *The Pirate, Waverley Novels,* vol. 24. Edinburgh: Robert Cadell, 1831.

———— *Tales and Romances of the Author of Waverley.* Edinburgh: Robert Cadell, 1833.

———— *The Poetical Works,* 4 vols. Edinburgh: Ballantyne, 1838.

———— 'Introductory Remarks on Popular Poetry'. In *The Lay of the Last Minstrel, and Marmion,* edited by J. G. Lockhart, 537–51. Edinburgh: Adam and Charles Black, 1869.

———— *The Letters of Sir Walter Scott,* edited by Herbert Grierson, 12 vols. London: Constable, 1932–1937.

———— *The Pirate,* edited Mark Weinstein and Alison Lumsden. Edinburgh: Edinburgh University Press, 2001.

Seward, Anna. *Llangollen Vale, with Other Poems.* London: G. Sael, 1796.

Shields, Juliette. *Sentimental Literature and Anglo-Scottish Identity, 1745–1820.* Cambridge: Cambridge University Press, 2010.

Simek, Rudolf. 'Monstra septentrionalia: Supernatural Monsters of the Far North in Medieval Lore'. In *Imagining the Supernatural North*, edited by Eleanor R. Barraclough, Danielle M. Cudmore and Stefan Donecker, 55–75. Edmonton: University of Alberta Press, 2016.

Simmons, Lucretia Van Tuyl. *Goethe's Lyric Poems in English Translation Prior to 1800*. Madison: Wisconsin University Studies, 1919.

Southey, Robert and Robert Lovel. *Poems: Containing the Retrospect, Odes, Elegies, Sonnets, &c.* London: C. Dilly, 1795.

Spooner, Catherine and Emma McEvoy. 'Gothic Locations'. In *The Routledge Companion to Gothic*, edited by Catherine Spooner and Emma McEvoy, 51–3. [reprinted] London: Routledge, 2009.

Stevens, Anne H. *British Historical Fiction before Scott*. Houndsmills: Palgrave, 2010.

Sterling, Joseph. *Poems*. London: G. G. J. & J. Robinson, 1789.

Summers, Montague. *A Gothic Bibliography*. Norderstedt: Books on Demand, 2020.

Sweet, Rosemary. *Antiquaries: The Discovery of the Past in Eighteenth-Century Britain*. London: Hambledon, 2004.

Syv, Peder, Ed. *Et Hundrede Udvalde danske Viser … Forøgede med det andet hundrede Viser*. Copenhagen: J. P. Bockenhoffer, 1739.

Tales of Terror. Dublin: John Brooke, 1801.

Taylor, George. *The French Revolution and the London Stage, 1789–1805*. Cambridge: Cambridge University Press, 2001.

Taylor, William. 'Ballad from the Original of J. W. von Goethe', *The Monthly Magazine* 6 (September 1798): 197.

———— *Historic Survey of German Poetry: Interspersed with Various Translations*, vol. 1. London: Treutel et al., 1830.

Temple, William. *An Introduction to the History of England*. London: R. & R. Simpson, 1695.

Thelwall, John. *Poems Chiefly Written in Retirement*. London: W. H. Parker, 1801.

Thomson, Douglass H. 'Mingled Measures: Gothic Parody in Tales of Wonder and Tales of Terror', *Romanticism and Victorianism on the Net* no. 50 (2008), https://id.erudit.org/iderudit/018143ar.

———— 'The Gothic Ballad'. In *New Companion to the Gothic*, edited by David Punter, 77–99. Hoboken, NJ: John Wiley & Sons, 2012.

Thompson, Gary Richard. *The Gothic Imagination: Essays in Dark Romanticism*. Washington: Washington State University, 1974.

Todorov, Tzvetan. *The Fantastic: A Structural Approach to a Literary Genre*. Ithaca, NY: Cornell University Press, 1975.

Townshend, Dale. 'Gothic Shakespeare'. In *A New Companion to the Gothic*, edited by David Punter, 38–63. Hoboken, NJ: John Wiley & Sons, 2012.

———— 'Shakespeare, Ossian and the Problem of "Scottish Gothic"'. In *Gothic Renaissance: A Reassessment*, edited by Elisabeth Bronfen and Beate Neumeier, 218–43. Manchester: Manchester University Press, 2014.

Troy, Maria Holmgren et al., Eds. *Nordic Gothic*. Manchester: Manchester University Press, 2020.

Wawn, Andrew. The Vikings and the Victorians: Inventing the Old North in Nineteenth-Century Britain. Cambridge: D. S. Brewer, 2000.

Warburton, William, Ed. *The Plays of William Shakespeare*, vol. 6. London: J. and P. Knapto et al., 1747.

Warton, Thomas. *The History of English Poetry, from the Close of the Eleventh to the Commencement of the Eighteenth Century*, vol. 1. London: J. Dodsley et al. 1774.

Watt, James. *Contesting the Gothic: Fiction, Genre, and Cultural Conflict, 1764–1832*. Cambridge: Cambridge University Press, 1999.

Winter, Jayne. 'International Traditions: Ballad Translations by Johann Gottfried Herder and Matthew Lewis', *German Life and Letters* 67, no. 1 (2014): 22–37.

Williams, Kelsey Jackson. 'Thomas Gray and the Goths: Philology, Poetry, and the Uses of the Norse Past in Eighteenth-Century England', *Review of English Studies* 65 (2014): 694–710.

——— *The Antiquary: John Aubrey's Historical Scholarship*. Oxford: Oxford University Press, 2016.

'The Wood Demon', *The New-England Magazine* (July 1833): 7.

Wordsworth, William. *Lyrical Ballads, with Other Poems*. London: T. N. Longman and O. Rees, 1800.

——— *The Poetical Works*, 5 vols. London: Longman, Rees, Orme, Brown and Green, 1827.

Anonymous Reviews in Periodicals (Listed by Year)

Review of *Runic Odes*. In *The Monthly Review* (December 1781): 426–27.

Review of *An Enquiry into the History of Scotland*. In *The Critical Review* (July 1790): 11–22.

Review of *Llangollen Vale*. In *The Analytical Review* (April 1796): 389.

Review of *The Monk*. In *The Monthly Review* (August 1797): 451.

Review of *Tales of Wonder*. In *The Anti-Jacobin Review* (March 1801): 322–23.

Review of *Tales of Wonder*. In the *Critical Review* (January 1802): 111–12.

Review of E. Lynn Linton's *The Lake Country*. In *British Quarterly Review* (April 1865): 476–95.

INDEX